Vision Quest;
A Time To Live

Vision Quest; A Time To Live

James Whaley

iUniverse, Inc.
Bloomington

Vision Quest; A Time To Live

iUniverse books may be ordered through booksellers or by contacting:

iUniverse
1663 Liberty Drive
Bloomington, IN 47403
www.iuniverse.com
1-800-Authors (1-800-288-4677)

ISBN: 978-1-4620-3643-1 (sc)
ISBN: 978-1-4620-3792-6 (ebk)

Printed in the United States of America

iUniverse rev. date: 07/20/2011

DEDICATION

I sincerely dedicate this work to my two grandchildren Roger and Madison. This is a fun story and I often thought of them as I wrote the tale. I love to tell stories and am especially glad to tell a story that I hope they will enjoy. I also want to acknowledge the support of other members of my family whose encouragement allows me to complete the task. Elinor, Kristi, Nisha, Jimmy, I love you all. May God bless.

PREFACE

At times when one is in a mood to write, an idea comes into your head. A picture appears and that is all you have. There is no plan; no story outline or diagram of what will be included, just a beginning. This is one of those stories that started and I went along for the ride. Most of the time I simply let the story tell itself. I mentioned to family members that I was anxious to get to the computer and find out what was going to happen that day with the story. This was one of those experiences that a writer enjoys. I had great fun with the hill country dialect of Pap and his family. I hope it is taken in the spirit it was written. As a former history teacher, I know that the strength of America is in the diversity of its people. I hope you enjoy the read as much as I enjoyed the write.

ACKNOWLEDGEMENTS

So many people have assisted me in reaching the level of writing I have achieved at this time. I appreciate the efforts they have given to teach me the skills and techniques of story telling. Thanks to the writing group that I have had the joy of being a part of for so many years. Thanks Dorothy, Joanne, Marvin, and Pat. A special thanks to Julie for the encouragement she has so often given my writing. A big thank you to Dorothy for the pain staking page by page review of this story. Her dedication to the art of writing is absolute and unselfish. Thanks to Ben Kilham for his work with black bears and allowing me to share with you some of his success. And thanks to those family members who allowed me more than my fair share of time on the computer. And finally but certainly not the least, to those who have read some of my work and expressed an appreciation of it. Your encouragement is what urged me on.

CHAPTER 1

Ruff, more formally known as Rufus Brindle, was a large man. His personality went hand in hand with his physical appearance. He had, however, earned his nickname through his speech, not his physical prowess. At a very early age he learned to get laughs from others when he was asked. "What's your name?" He would answer by pronouncing only the first part of his name "Ruff." Over the years his voice changed into a deep guttural resonance that vibrated as it passed through his throat, and the nickname stuck. Ruff always talked like a bear standing guard over a newly claimed meal, but his name also echoed his fearlessness in a desire to try anything and everything at least once before his life was over. Whether it was sky diving, hang-gliding, surfing, rock climbing, mud wrestling or white-water river rafting, Ruff loved it all. Anything out of doors, anything to challenge what the natural wilderness had to offer, he tested himself on it all. He particularly enjoyed the rugged, untamed foothills of the Colorado Rockies.

For the 12th of June, the weather was mild. The heat spells that were usually expected during this time of year had yet to materialize. Ruff had said it was perfect camping weather—a great time to get outdoors and see what Mother Nature had to offer.

He had reserved a camping spot in the Roosevelt National Forest located in north central Colorado. Roosevelt was a mountainous area of the Rockies foothills on the eastern side of the continental divide located in Larimer County. The campsite was a picturesque spot in the upper valley of the Cache la Poudre and Big Thompson Rivers. The area was a thickly forested area of the Poudre Canyon. He liked the area because of its rugged terrain, plus being located in the Canyon Lakes Ranger District where his good friend Bill Waddle was district superintendent. Being of similar personalities, they occasionally engaged themselves in playing a joke on one another. Several years ago, when Bill knew Ruff had a reservation in the Canyon Lakes District, he had issued an alert on Ruff as a drunk lost in one of the many canyons that dotted the region. He used the ruse as an official training exercise for a newly organized search and rescue team. He informed the rescue team only that Ruff, a harmless and well-known drunk, frequented the area and had become lost. The potential problems with his realistic training activity included the fact that he failed to inform Ruff about the exercise. And since no notification came to the search party, if his friend reacted as he expected him to, the team would undoubtedly believe they had a belligerent drunk on their hands. Ruff reacted as expected and the rescue squad put their training to work. Ruff had planned a day of river kayaking and refused to go with them as a 'lost and found' camper so they did what they were trained to do. They wrestled him to the ground, handcuffed him and took him to the district superintendent's office for processing. Only then did Bill make his appearance and let Ruff, along with the rescue team, know the truth about the exercise. Bill Waddle was the only one involved that found humor in the story he told, especially the way Bill liked to tell the tale.

As one sector of Roosevelt National Forest, the Canyon Lakes District was part of an immense area encompassing some 814,000 acres and over 1200 square miles. Having camped there many times Ruff knew the area as well as he knew his home neighborhood in Colorado Springs. He arranged a five-night reservation in the Roosevelt, plenty of time to complete his plan for Mike.

Although he was nearing his sixty-first birthday, he was still an avid camper and wilderness fanatic. He had undertaken this trip to try to do what he felt needed to be done for his Sister Jennifer's youngest child. Being a single parent, Jennie Anderson, as she was better known, had three grown girls, Susan, Linda, and Jill—all out of the home and on their own. However, her pride and joy, was her nineteen-year-old son Michael. Jennie had fought tooth and toenail with the three girls as they progressed through their teens. Both the girls and their mother admitted that the four of them fought like a den of wildcats as the sisters were growing up. But with Mike it had been a different story. He turned out to be her dream child. Always the polite one who possessed a positive personality, never causing her any problems and willing to help with the household chores. If she asked him to spend his evening reorganizing the kitchen cabinets or rearranging the living room furniture, an objection rarely came. But there was a part of Mike that bothered Ruff, as certain facets of Mike's makeup were confusing to his uncle. When Ruff said anything to Jennie about Mike's lack of desire to participate in outdoor activities, or to get involved in any type of physical contests, or vigorous behavior, she would laugh it off and admonish Ruff for his aggressiveness. She would remind her brother that Mike's interests were just different, a complete opposite of Ruff and that created some feelings of jealousy.

Ruff agreed with her in part. Mike's slight of build physical apperence, his introverted personality, and his reluntance to participate in unfamiliar activities, definitely clashed with Ruff's belief of how a nineteen-year-old should act.

But Ruff vehemently denied the jealous charge. However, Jennie would insist that there existed one aspect of Mike that Ruff couldn't begin to equal and therefore couldn't accept, and Ruff knew it.

Mike was an avid reader and in his second year of college at Fort Collins. He carried a 4.0 GPA in his undergraduate studies in Social Pathology. Ruff, on the other hand, never finished high school. Having dropped out after two incomplete years of being in and out of the classroom. But, Ruff knew the out of doors, and he loved it. He was anxious to expose Mike to his outdoor world.

"Let's get a move on, boy," growled Ruff, "we're burning daylight and we've got a ways to go yet."

As he spoke Ruff, glanced over his shoulder to see Mike wearily trying to climb over a large boulder; his pack hung much too low on his back. "Put some muscle into it, son, you got to keep up," yelled Ruff.

Mike never looked up, never responded, but awkwardly continued his struggle up the steep slope.

Ruff had little trouble convincing his sister to let him take Mike on the weekend hiking trip in the foothills of the Rockies of northern Colorado. She knew that Ruff had a vast history in living in the wilderness and a wealth of knowledge about camping in the wild. She also had Ruff's word that he would never allow anything bad to happen to his nephew. Not even at the risk of his own life, he promised her, would he permit that to occur. At first, Mike refused to go. Then his mother gave him a choice: "Either go with your uncle, or fly with me to visit your Aunt Carol, in Portland." She knew her offer would leave her son with no choice at all. There were two reasons: First of all he feared flying, and when he did, had to double up on the Dramamine to calm the anxiety attacks. In addition to flying, he could barely tolerate the behavior of his mother's sister. Persistent in her attempts of trying to get a hug, Aunt Carol constantly badgered him about his lack of a love life.

Acting on his own choices, Mike suggested he could stay home by himself. To this solution neither his mother nor his Uncle Ruff would hear of it.

"You got to get out, boy. A day without a memory is a day wasted. You got to get with nature, find out what the world is made of, have some experiences, live a little. You got to give yourself something to remember when you get my age."

Now standing amid the tall pines, Ruff adjusted the oversized camp pack and turned once again to encourage the young man. "Got to step on it, Mike. It's another hard two hours to the campsite I planned for us tonight."

Mike groaned, and it made him blush because it came out louder than he had intended. "We've already been going strong for over an hour now. Let's take a break," he pleaded.

"The first leg of any hike is always the toughest. You're doing great. Don't let up now."

About a half-hour before sunset they finally reached the campsite. A pleasant place, a little clearing along side a tributary of the Cache la Poudre River and a fair-sized mountain stream.

"This should do nicely," Ruff said proudly. He looked around creating the layout of the camp in his mind. The rest of the evening went as well as expected with Ruff barking directions and Mike mechanically responding. The tent went up swiftly and Ruff started lining the campfire site with boulders found along the streambed. As he constructed tripods over the fire site to support a kettle, he sent Mike into the woods to collect "dry wood so it won't smoke us out of house and home," Ruff instructed. After a filling meal, they leaned back on their pack frames and Ruff began reminiscing about the time he came face to face with a bear a few years earlier while camping in the area.

"If you ever encounter a black bear in this country, remember this, he or she, is a highly intelligent animal. But all bears don't respond to people the same. However, wild black bears seldom attack people unless they feel threatened. Usually, if you stand still and let the bear identify you it will probably leave. If you speak to it, talk in a normal tone and make sure it has a clear escape route, then it doesn't feel cornered. If the bear stands up on its hind legs and isn't growling, which by the way they seldom do, it is just trying to get a better look at you. If the bear huffs, pops its jaws, or stomps the ground, it just wants you to give it space. So back away and keep your eyes on the bear. If the bear approaches you, it could be a camp bear looking for a hand out. Wave your hands over your head and stand your ground. Yell to discourage it from coming closer. If you must, pick up rocks and throw them at the bear. However, if you see cubs with—"

Interrupting with a disgusted tone, Mike's comment was curt, "This is sounding more and more like one of your lectures."

Ruff laughed. "I reckon so. But you need to know just the same." The quiet engulfed them as they listened to the night sounds. On occasion, Ruff would make a brief comment, such as: "Bobcat, I suspect." Or, "Hear that night hawk overhead?" Mike never answered his uncle. Ruff finally surrendered to the silence and they turned in for the night.

When Mike awoke the following morning, the sun appeared high in the sky, with Ruff nowhere around. Finding the coals of last night's fire still warm, he threw on a few sticks to get the fire going. Putting some water on to heat for his malt-o-meal, Mike waited for his uncle's return. It would be a long anxious wait.

First testing the water in the stream thinking he might go wading, but quickly decided the water was much too cold. Then Mike decided to hike back up the trail by which they came the night before, but because of the dense woods, he began to become concerned that he might get lost. Finally he settled for spending the day reading one of the three books stuffed in his backpack when Ruff wasn't watching him pack. Ruff wasn't much on reading, especially on a camping trip.

Mike suddenly noticed the sun getting low in the western sky and still no sign of Ruff. He stoked the campfire, put some water in the kettle, and heated one of the prepared food pouches. When night fell and darkness surrounded the little fire, he became uneasy and built the fire up to compensate for his anxiety. Various shadows of eerie shapes and images danced around the perimeter of the camp, he crept into the tent, leaving the front tent flap open so he could see the fire in its pit, and bundled into the confines of his sleeping bag, fretfully waited for the unknown. It seemed like hours before he finally dropped off into an uneasy sleep. *He was riding a train; he could hear the rumble of the locomotive and an occasional clackity clack of the wheels. And the air, the air rushing past at a fierce rate. A large half-opened window beside his head allowed the air to rush in, then the train started picking up speed. The wind rushed past his ears faster, faster. Suddenly the rail car collapsed; something heavy started crushing the rail car.*

Mike suddenly came awake. The sides of the tent were being buffeted by strong winds. The front tent flap whipped wildly in the wind. The rain began with huge drops striking the tent, and then it came in a steady downpour. After securing the front tent flap, Mike huddled in the waterproof shelter of the tent for much of the morning before the storm slowly moved on to drench new territory. When Mike finally braved the outdoors he found the campfire a miniature swimming pool, and the nearby wood he had collected soaked through. He relocated the fire pit to higher ground and lined it with the rocks as he had watched Ruff do the night before. Overnight the air turned much colder, his fingers were becoming numb as he searched for anything that would help him start a fire. He discovered that in areas protected by over hanging rock layers, relatively dry wood could be found. With the help of some matches and tissue paper he found in one of the packs, he soon had a blazing fire going. Though by then he was exhausted and half-frozen.

With the sun overhead, he sat on the damp ground eating a second container of beef stew in as many meals, he became aware of another presence. Turning his head slowly, he saw two bear cubs meandering down the very trail he and Ruff had taken. In between batting each other with their heads, the two cubs sniffed the air. *Not really cubs, they are too large to be called cubs.* He felt a little ashamed when he realized he was talking to himself. Without moving, he traced their path with his eyes. *They're coming this way. They will smell the food! What do I do? I know I am not supposed to run, but they smell the food and if they get any closer they will see me!*

Then he saw her. The old sow. She moved with a slight limp from her left front paw, following some twenty yards behind the cubs. It looked as though she had recently been in a battle, for her fur was scraggly and covered in spots with mud. She ambled slowly after the cubs. Then one of the cubs snorted loudly and immediately the other two bears came to attention. Mike had dropped the container of beef stew on himself when he first saw the cubs and they apparently had picked up Mike's scent, or rather the scent of the beef stew, separating it from the many odors coming from the camp. Moving slowly, Mike grabbed a firebrand from the campfire. Holding it out in front, he jumped up beside a large pine, hoping to keep the tree between him and the bears. All three bears were now woofing and growling among themselves as they watched Mike. One of the cubs gave a snort and made a lazy half-hearted lunge toward Mike. With an awkward swing Mike struck the cub square across the nose with the hot club. Whining, the cub backed away swiping at its nose with a paw. He gave Mike one last woof, turned and trotted down along the creek. The other cub and the old sow found Mike's fresh stew container on the ground. Each of the bears tried to stick their nose into the container and tore it apart, then began foraging through the camp. Most of their attention seemed to be on the campfire and neither made any attempt to get past it. Fortunately, Mike's food was double sealed and stashed in the camp pack that in turn hung high from an overhanging tree branch as Ruff had instructed. Mike realized that he was holding his breath and let out a lung full of air, both surprised and relieved that except for the one cub, the bears appeared unconcerned with his presence. Not being able to pick up the scent of the cached food, and finding nothing else of interest, the two bears meandered along down the shore of the stream following the route of the lead cub. They were nearly out of sight before Mike felt brave enough to toss the firebrand back into the fire. He added more wood to the fire and longed for a re-appearance of his uncle. Where had Ruff gone and what had happened to him?

CHAPTER 2

Mike pulled the ground cloth out of the tent and spread it beside the large fire. Then placing his sleeping bag on it, he set to work collecting a large amount of reasonably dry wood, and stacked it nearby. Between worrying about bears and keeping the fire burning high, Mike spent a very fretful night. He finally fell into a deep sleep a couple of hours before sunrise.

He awoke late as he had the first day, only this morning the sun was high and shining in his face. The ground cloth and sleeping bag were damp with the morning dew, so he set to work stretching a length of rope between two trees and hanging them both over it so the sun and breeze could dry them out. After fixing himself a meal of overcooked pancakes and well-done, pan-fried microwave bacon, he decided to heat some water to wash his dirty pots and pans. After re-building the tripods destroyed by the encounter with the bears, Mike placed a pot of water on the spit across the fire, then returned to the stream to wash himself. The water was terribly cold, but he succeeded in washing his upper body and changed into a clean shirt. During his chore of caring for the needs of the campsite, he convinced himself that he should do some exploring along the stream and into the woods in hopes of finding some trace of his uncle. He had located a rock ledge along one side of the stream in his earlier search for dry wood, and wanted to take a closer look at it. He figured that as long as he stayed near the stream he could find his way back to the campsite. The first task before leaving the campsite would be to make certain that his food pack was well out of the reach of the bears should they decide to return for a second helping.

That done, he packed a small knapsack, strapped a hunting knife around his belt and set out. Not knowing the area and unaware of what lie ahead worried Mike considerably. Where am I going, and what am I going to? Deciding to head up stream, he started out. After traveling a couple of miles from the campsite, Mike realized that at some point, he had to search the woods for some sign of his uncle. Not wanting to lose his way among the trees, he collected several dozen marble-sized pebbles along the stream, which he planned to place in the center of a mound of dirt he would scoop up along the way, one mound just in sight of another. Some would have to be close together, others quite far apart. He once read where an early trail had been mapped out this way. He picked out a high ridge as his destination, and set forth. Once there he could holler for Ruff, and if no success would still have time to return to camp before dark.

As the hours passed the ridge didn't seem to be getting much closer, and Mike was feeling the effects of hiking up and down the small valleys hidden by the trees. While crossing a small clearing, Mike knelt to the ground, and prepared to plant one of the small pebbles. Suddenly, he heard the loud report of a gun, then another. From the sound, he knew whoever was shooting, was very close. Startled, Mike dropped flat to the ground and froze. Listening intently, he heard human voices coming from somewhere not too far away. Squirming his way out of the clearing and back into the protection of the trees and underbrush, he lay still for several minutes. The voices continued, and slowly Mike began to detect their direction. *There are people around; maybe they know something about Ruff. Maybe one of the voices is Ruff.* Quietly Mike crept toward the direction of the voices.

"I's tote ya I's sees em. I's tote ya, did'dent I's?"

"Ya did Pap. Ya tote we'ens rite."

Mike couldn't understand what they were saying so silently he crept around a large boulder and peered through the brush, there appeared to be two figures. He couldn't see faces or determine their age, as they both wore Australian style large brimmed hats pulled low on their heads. However, one looked to be not much more than a boy and certainly younger than Mike. They were both tall and thin, and dressed in dark overalls. Mike had seen photographs of earlier farmers that wore the same type of clothing.

"Now wot? Pap. Wot we'ens do wit em?" It was the younger one that spoke.

"Weel I's rec'on we'ens need ta skin em out rite 'ear. We'ens need ta work fast ef"in some one 'ear the shot. Best git wit it, boy."

All Mike could see were the two figures standing beside a dark clump on the ground just a few feet in front of them. He decided to move to his left to another boulder that would give him a much better view of the two people. He didn't want to show himself until he was sure it was safe. Adjusting his knapsack on his back, and checking to make sure the hunting knife was secure in his belt, he crouched low, creeping to the second boulder. His left foot hit a dead twig on the ground and it snapped.

"Wot was thet? Did ya 'ear thet, boy? I's 'ear somptin. Thet ya makin thet noise, boy?"

"I's did'dent do nothin, Pap. Ya jest a mite jumpity ever since ya sees'em."

"Weel, lets git these done an git out of 'ear."

Mike peeked out from behind the boulder; suddenly he realized what the two were doing. *It's a bear! They shot a bear! They can't do that. Ruff said the bears here were protected. This is a national park. No hunting of any kind is allowed here.* Mike slipped behind the boulder and leaned his back against it. *They're skinning out a bear that they shot illegally! Hey, they're poachers.* Mike peered around the boulder for the second time and watched the two at work. *That's what they are, all right. They shot a bear and—wait a minute, what's that kid doing? There's another. Another bear. They shot two of them. They shot two bears. Wait, I can see them now, it's the cubs, the ones from last night, and they shot the cubs!*

Mike wheeled back around the boulder. With his back pressed tightly against the rock, his mind reeled and his breathing became rapid. It all came together for him now. *The man and boy had killed two legally protected bears. They were guilty of breaking the law. They were poachers and it would not set kindly with them to know that they had been spotted while in the process of committing a federal crime.* He needed to get out of the area, and he needed to get out now.

It was all Mike could do to keep himself from jumping up and running back through the woods to the stream. *Ruff, where are you when I need you the most?*

CHAPTER 3

Lowering his field glasses, Ruff broke into a broad grin and almost laughed out loud when Mike smacked the cub with the firebrand. *The boy has guts. Either that or downright foolish.* Ruff added the second thought when he realized that Mike probably didn't know that the bears were camp bears which usually weren't dangerous unless you were dumb enough to get between them and food. Actually, Ruff had been more worried about the old sow than the cubs. It was easy to see that she had been in a tussle. Probably with a male bear after one of the cubs. Nothing will rile an old sow mother more than an old boar after her offspring. Mike had been lucky, because if the old sow had set her mind to it, Mike would not have been able to discourage her as easily as the cub. Ruff lowered the rifle he had held at his shoulder, ready to put a shot at the bear's feet if need be. He had obtained a special permit to carry the firearm in the National Forest, thanks to the assistance of his buddy Bill. From atop the huge granite boulder he stood on, Ruff watched as Mike busied himself with the campfire.

Ruff hadn't planned on the bears. His intent had been to let Mike make the right decisions around the camp and to give the boy a chance to find his own way in an unfamiliar setting. He knew he was playing a risky game, and Mike could have to pay dearly for any mistake he made. Ruff knew the boy had it in him, he just needed to test himself. Ruff had come up with the idea that the boy needed to go on a vision quest much like many of the Native American societies once used to test an adolescent boy. If the boy passed the test the tribe would accept him as a man. It often developed into a dangerous adventure then, and Ruff knew it could be dangerous now. Ruff squatted on the boulder and watched Mike rearrange his camp. *Good idea, Mike, bears don't like fire and bunking down near the fire is smart.*

Feeling a rumble in his own belly, Ruff decided his nephew would be safe for the time being and stood to stretch. *Might as well slip back to my own camp and grab a bite. I need to bear proof it a little with Mama and her kids around.*

Ruff, trying to catch a last fleeting glimpse of his nephew, became distracted for a fleeting moment, and as he stepped back to descend the boulder his boot hit a patch of green wet moss. At first the worn tread of the boot held but as Ruff put more pressure and weight on it, the boot slipped. Ruff went down hard on his back. With the wind knocked out of him, he slid down the side of the large boulder doing a three-quarter spin. As he came to a stop, his head struck a smaller rock. Ruff had not uttered a sound, and unfortunately, no one was around to hear the sharp crack of Ruff's head against the rock. Ruff did not move, the blow had rendered him unconscious.

The sun, directly over head, shined into Ruff's eyes when he opened them sometime later. For a moment, his body seemed paralyzed. He tested his feet and found he could move his legs. Then he tried his arms by bringing his left arm up to his head. *So far so good. What the sam-hill happened? How long have I been here?* Questions raced through Ruff's mind. He pulled his hand away from his head and for the first time fear spread through his body as he looked at the blood on his hand. *What kind of dumb stunt have I pulled here? I need to get up.* As Ruff braced himself with his hands, he started to raise his head. Pain ripped through him like a gunshot. His head began to spin like a child's top and his eyes would not come into focus. His world crashed as the blackness folded in around him and again he disappeared in the realm of unconsciousness. Ruff would not be available to aid Mike any time soon. Survival was fast becoming an issue which would need to be met by each man, using his own abilities.

CHAPTER 4

When Ruff awoke for the second time since his fall, it was in the dark of night. It took him several minutes to remember where he was. He didn't need to see the area to know he was on a ledge where he had spent many hours studying the horizon. This part of the Roosevelt National Forest was familiar territory to him. He had explored and camped in this region more times than he could count since his first experience when only ten years old. The problem wasn't one of where he was; the problem was why he was here. A part of his brain seemingly wasn't working. His memory seemed to be malfunctioning. What day was it and how long had he been on the ledge? All these questions continued to flow through his mind, and the more they spun around in his brain the more confused he became. In addition to his confusion, every time he moved his head, the shooting pain reminded him of the fact that it hurt something fierce. What had happened? When he touched the back of his head on the left side he groaned. He must have hit his head doing—doing what? He tried to set up and yelped as a stab of pain shot through his left ankle. Forcing himself up into a sitting position his head immediately began to spin, and before he could lay his torso back down to a prone position, his mind disappeared into another black abyss.

Unknowingly, in his condition, Ruff had more trouble than he could ever imagine. In hitting his head he suffered a concussion. And if he could look into a mirror while awake he would notice that his pupils were unequally dilated. As so often occurs with accidents such as this, memory loss is common. Ruff had no recall of the event leading to his fall and the resulting concussion. When and if that memory returned, would be something Ruff could not answer even if he had the expertise to ask the question. The condition of the ankle was another matter entirely. It might take some of his weight, but not for long and it could take several weeks to heal.

When Ruff awoke for the third time, his eyes once again looked into a full sun high overhead. It took some time before he could keep his left eye open for any length of time. His mental condition had not changed. He knew where he was but not what he was doing there. Again he tried to set up and eventually was successful even though any quick movement sent his head into a tailspin. As best he could, he examined his ankle. The swelling told him that he had a bad sprain. Having suffered from ankle sprains before, and he knew that this one was bad enough to require accepting severe pain if and when weight were put on it.

Ruff suddenly became aware of the factor of time. He seemed to have a great concern about how much time had elapsed while he was out. Why did that seem so important? Why did it matter? Did he expect to be somewhere at a certain time? Could someone be waiting for him somewhere? Biting his lip in frustration at not being able to answer any of his own questions, he became aware of how dry his mouth seemed to be.

Ruff was familiar with the out of doors and knew from his thirst that it had been some time since his last drink of water. One glance at the sun determined that it was about an hour into the afternoon. Which afternoon? He thought to himself. In the daylight he examined the ground around him and noticed for the first time that he seemed to be well equipped for spending at least a day out in the open country. His pack was on his back, a canteen on his belt, which he immediately checked and found to be almost full, and a ground cloth that could be used as shelter or warmth, he also had a favorite hunting knife. But the rifle he carried had flown from his hands when he fell and slipped into a bramble bush. It went undetected in his haphazard search. Within crawling distance he noticed his camping/fishing hat. The brown one with the broad rim and soft lining that felt comfortable on him. His first attempt of moving to retrieve the hat pained him to the point that it took more than he could accept. Struggling out of the straps of his pack, he searched it and found a container of aspirin. Taking several and shoving them in his mouth he took a large swig of water from the canteen, then started to take another when the out-doors-man-ship he possessed stopped him. *No telling how long this might have to last me*, he thought. Making a second try for his hat, he managed to be successful. Putting it on his head carefully, he smiled slightly. Good old camping hat, he thought.

CAMP! The word exploded into his head. *I must have a camp somewhere! Somewhere near. I have no change of clothes with me, no cooking utensils, and no sleeping bag. Also no food except for some dried turkey and my favorite pecan-dried prune-raisin trail mix. I must have a camp near by. But in what direction? I could never find it, I know myself well enough to know it is well hidden and someone would have to step on it to find it. TRUST YOUR INSTINCTS! That is what he always told groups of folks that he spoke to from time to time. "If you are in an unfamiliar situation or place, trust your instincts to find a way out." His own words were mocking him. But he knew they were true. All I have to do is let my mind go, let my inner self and my sub conscience take over. Let it tell me which way to go. I may have to crawl, but I'll get there, wherever there is!*

Ruff looked around, he hoped to locate some sort of support he could use as a crutch, but he spotted nothing. So he secured his belongings to his belt and body, crawling by pulling himself along with a military type elbow and knee crawl. He paid no heed to what direction he was going, letting his sub conscience take him where it wanted.

CHAPTER 5

Letting his first instinct pass, Mike sat frozen to the spot behind the boulder. *If I don't run, what do I do?* He asked himself. *I can't just stay here and wait to be discovered! Where is Ruff? He would know what to do. What would Ruff do? Probably just stand up and face these two—poachers. That's what they are, and if caught they know they will be fined and probably go to jail. They won't want that to happen. Maybe Ruff would slip back into the woods and make it to the stream and back to camp. No, Ruff wouldn't run off, he'd probably face these guys.*

"Hay Pap, Look wot I's found." Someone beside him yelled out. Mike's head jerked to the left at the sound. So distracted by his own thoughts, he had not noticed a third person who was now standing beside a tree holding a double barrel shotgun pointed right at him.

"Don't be a bother, I's bout got this varmint skinned up." The older man never looked up from his task of removing the hide from the cub bear.

"Pap, I's tink ya want ta take a look et this," answered the man with the shotgun. "I's got me a spy."

The older man looked up. All he could see was the man with the shotgun. Because of the boulder, he couldn't see Mike. "Wot ya talkin bout Will? Wot spy?"

The man holding the shotgun motioned for Mike to stand up by bouncing the muzzle end of the gun up and down. Mike shakily obeyed, but because his legs were so weak he nearly collapsed before he steadied himself enough to stand. With a surprised look on his face the older man said,

"Well I's be horn swaggled, wot ya done got holt of boy." The older man ambled over and glaring nose to nose spat out his words squarely in Mike's face, "who are ya and wot are ya doin 'ear boy?"

Mike was petrified and too scared to respond. "An'sir me boy, an do it now!" The old man insisted, moving his face even closer to Mike.

Scared to death, Mike moved away from that face, then peered toward the shotgun once again and answered meekly but with more steadiness in his voice than he expected. "I—I wasn't doing anything, just exploring."

"Wot we'ens ta do wit em, Pap? The youngest of the three joined the others. Mike jumped a little at the sound of the voice so close behind him.

"I's rec'on he's jest half ta come wit we'ens till I's dee'side wot we'ens got 'ear. Sides he's ken help we'ens tote some of the bar." With that the old man poked a finger into Mike's chest and motioned for him to move over to where the two slain, and now skinned, cubs lay.

"We'ens need ta finish dressin out these varmints. We'ens fix a travois ta haul out our vittles."

The old man seemed mostly talking to himself. He quickly slit the under belly of one of the cubs and proceeded to drag the entrails out of the body cavity.

"Ham, ya go ahead an take care of the other one, an Will, ya sat thet youn'un down 'ear so's I's ken sees em an ya make the travois."

The older boy Will shoved Mike to a sitting position and with the muzzle of the shotgun motioned for him to stay put. The three poachers knew what they were doing, and in a matter of minutes the two cubs were field dressed and mounted on the tripod like sled.

Each of the "boys" had a makeshift harness on his back and when they tested their loads, they hefted them with little expression, but Mike thought that each of the cubs must have been over 150 pounds. Mike was instructed to carry a load by wrapping one of the hides of a cub around his shoulders and the old man did the same with the other one. Mike was somewhat surprised when they started off in a direction away from the stream, and then up one of the many valleys in the region. Mike tried to keep track of the directions they took as they made their journey but soon became confused when he realized they were moving back down the trail they had just traversed.

Then he remembered something Ruff had described once. *They were backtracking.* They were going back over their own tracks then moving forward in a different direction, being careful not to expose their movement by leaving any signs of what they had done. No one spoke as they traveled and it was nearly dark when they came upon a crude cabin located at the end of one of the valleys. Mike had no idea how far they were from the mountain stream where his camp was located, but they had traveled the distance in less than a day.

The cabin was well hidden under a rock overhang at the edge of a little clearing that was bounded on three sides by steep wooded inclines. *A box canyon* thought Mike, *one way in, one way out. This is not a place that would be easy to see, or to find. I wonder if it is legal to live in a National Forest? Maybe I don't want to know!*

CHAPTER 6

Mike had been at the cabin for two days now and except for the first night. remained confined to his limited world only by the word of Will. According to Will Mike must stay in the area of a small shed some 25 yards and slightly downhill from the cabin. Will had told him that if the ground got too cold, to crawl in the shed to sleep. Will pointed out to him that if Mike got too far away from the shed it would be Will that he would have to answer to. Will, didn't bother to tell him how far was too far. Mike had talked to no one and knew little more than when he first saw the cabin. Apparently Pap, the two boys, and a lady called Emma, lived in the small cabin. Mike couldn't imagine it having more than one room from the size of it. An older woman Emma spent most of her time in the cabin. On occasion, she would come out side to fetch wood, or to boil some water in the big kettle near the corner of the cabin. Now and then she also made a trip to the outhouse which served as a bathroom, located behind and on the other side of the cabin. About five feet tall, and a very slim build, Emma had dark hair as did the two sons. All four of them had the same expressionless facial appearance, and Mike wondered if Emma could be the wife of Pap. Mike didn't see anything of the old man from the time he entered the cabin shortly after they arrived. Mike passed the days by spending much of the first day watching Will and Ham scrape the two bear hides. They had mounted them on boards and hung the mounts on the side of the cabin that faced in Mike's direction.

As the two "boys" worked, they rarely spoke. There was only an occasional grunt, giving of directions, or a comment on progress, but nothing told of a relationship. From Mike's thinking he assumed they had scraped similar hides many times before. The second day began with a brief rain shower and Mike spent the morning in the shed. Mike surmised that "Pap" was the father of the two boys, Will being several years older than Ham, but he had no knowledge of the relationship of Emma to the rest of the family.

Emma was an anomaly. The first morning at the cabin after his "capture," Emma had wandered down to where he sat. Without introduction or fanfare, she asked, "how old 'ear ya boy?"

Not knowing what else to do, Mike answered. "Nineteen."

"Ya yonger en Will an older en Ham."

"I thought I might be. How old are you?"

"Ya don't esk thet of a lady."

When Mike didn't say anything she spoke again, "Ya tink I's a lady?"

"Yes ma'am, Yes I do." Mike wondered what was going through her mind. *You never know when an adversary might become a much-needed friend.* Mike remembered one of Ruff's often-repeated statements.

Emma presented just a hint of a smile. "I's got ta go. I's got work ta do. Ya wont ta help we'ens work?"

"Yes ma'am. Yes I do." Mike answered.

Without another word, Emma turned and walked briskly back to the cabin and went inside without once looking back in Mike's direction.

The first night Will had chained him to a tree beside the shed with a dog chain. During the night he started wondering what had happened to the dog; he had the feeling that he was taking the place of the dog. The second night Will explained to Mike that he wasn't going to the trouble of chaining him up. If Mike went anywhere away from the cabin and didn't get himself lost in the woods, a mountain lion or she-bear would most likely find him. And he would end up as their food for the night. "So's my a'vice to ya is ta stay put." Will admonished.

Something else Mike had learned about the occupants of the cabin concerned food. So far as Mike knew, food consisted of either a stew or hash made out of some kind of mystery meat, that Mike didn't think he wanted to know about, mixed with greens and either potatoes or turnips. Whatever it's origin of the meat, it needed tenderizing and also needed to be cooked for a longer time than Emma seemed to allow.

The morning stew was the same as the evening stew. There was no noon stew for which he was thankful. No one had bothered him and he assumed they were pretty confident that he wasn't going anywhere. Where would he go? He didn't know where he was, so how would he know which way was back to camp? Anyway, one of them could undoubtedly catch him before he got very far.

Yet, he somehow knew that he had to make some kind of plan for getting away from his captors. So far they had not threatened him. It was as if they didn't know what to do with him. But they might decide to do him harm at any time. Successful or not he had to make a break and try to find the stream.

And what of Ruff, if he came back to camp, how long would he hang around, before "pulling up stakes and moving out," as he would say.

Okay, lets' say I commit to leaving, what do I need? I still have my hunting knife, they never did bother taking that from me. I don't think I have anything in my pocket. He checked his pockets. *Hey, I have that little compass on that magnifying glass that I picked up at Wal-mart, I can determine direction. The only other thing is a handkerchief. Now, what don't I have? I don't have a map, no food, no water, and no idea where I am going. This will be a cinch. I guess I'll just have to get some of those things.*

*   *   *

In the days that followed, Mike refined his plan. First he searched the area around his little world and located a jar with a lid that had a finger hold near the top, that could serve as a canteen, *and he could even attach it to his belt.* He hid it under the little shed that served as his bedroom. Since it was the only thing on the menu, his food would have to be stew. He needed something he could save some of this mystery meat in.

What if I set the chunks of meat and larger pieces of potato or turnip out in the sun and let them sun dry? Then I could store them in one of my socks. I need to figure out some way to wash the sock first. If I had water and food, I would need to know the when and where. I could leave right after dark but it doesn't get dark until late this time of the year. What about when the men go hunting? They left Emma watching me when they took off yesterday to hunt game. I could slip away from Emma, even if she noticed I was missing, they wouldn't find out until they returned. And if it was dark when they returned that might give me several more hours' head start!

About a week or so later, (he had lost track of just how many days he had been at the cabin) when Will approached him with his evening stew or hash, or whatever the devil it might be called, Mike was about to ask him how long they intended to keep him prisoner when Will spoke. "This 'ears the last of the bar meat. Pap sez we'ens got ta git game. I's want ya ta be'havf ya'self whilst we'ens out. Emma'll fix ya somptin in the mornin. We'ens leaf be'fer daybreak." And without waiting for any reply from Mike, he turned and slowly sauntered back to the cabin.

Bear meat! He had been eating the cub meat! Hey! This may be my chance; I could leave as soon as it gets dark. Will said they'd leave before daybreak, they won't bother to check on me. By the time Emma brings me breakfast, I will be long gone. I need to fill my water bottle, force myself to eat this stew and collect this mornings stew that is drying beside the shed and get ready to leave. Mike's mind was racing a mile a minute, trying to think of everything and wondering if his plan would work. *Well you have to try boy; you have to give yourself a chance. Go for it.* He imagined he heard Ruff speaking.

It was about a half-hour after sunset that Mike saw from the gap below the cabin door, the faint light of a candle go out in the cabin. He waited another half-hour and then quietly began his exit from the canyon. *I wonder what they would do if they catch me.* Mike seemed to know it wouldn't be pretty. He tried to remember everything Ruff had told him about traveling in the woods.

Don't get in too big of a hurry, a sprained ankle does you no good. Move quickly and quietly. A lot of noise just attracts the attention of what ever might be within earshot. Keep your eyes on the Sun, moon, or a star, so you know what direction your going. Don't be afraid to go around an obstacle, but recheck your direction afterwards to align yourself with the way you want to go.

Watch for animal trails, following them can be dangerous if it is being used by a predator while you are traveling on it, but an animal trail will lead you to water eventually. Plus animals usually travel the path of least resistance. Just watch out for overhangs as most animal trail's don't yell 'duck'

Mike tried to check the little compass, it was difficult to see in the dark, but he thought he was traveling east. *I know this is the way we came into the valley, he told himself, and I know that we crossed a high ridge just before traveling up the valley. If I can find that ridge I will know when to turn. I think we turned north after crossing the ridge, so I need to turn south. Where I go from there I have no idea. We'll see what happens.*

CHAPTER 7

Ruff rested in the shade of a small bush. Exhausted from the exertion of crawling across rock and brush, Ruff tried to determine how far his effort had taken him. *I am making better head way than expected, what with this ankle throbbing even though I have made every attempt at not trying to push himself with my left foot.* But on occasion he would be forced to use the sore ankle to climb over one of the many rock ledges he had to transcend. It had been over half a day since he awoke for the third time. Ruff had been somewhat successful in his attempt to keep his mind free of trying to predetermine his direction. He wanted his sub-conscience to lead the way. While resting, he allowed himself one sip of water from the canteen. Shading his eyes with his hand, for the sun was still very bright in his left eye, he peered across the grassy clearing to his left. It seemed devoid of life but he knew it could house any number of small animals. He needed something to eat besides what little of his trail mix he had consumed. With a quick rub of his sore elbows, he pulled himself around the small bush and started through the grassy clearing. Suddenly he became very dizzy and he felt a sharp excruciating pain on left side of his head. He groaned and the blackness came over him for a fourth time.

Some time later as he came to, Ruff's head slowly cleared. *Voices, that's what I hear, it's voices. I hear voices.*

"Wot ya tink, Pap?" The younger son, Ham asked the question.

"I's tink he's had his heed bashed in, thet's wot I's tink."

"Enny thin we'ens ken do fer him? Pap." Will chimed in.

"Not likely, he's got a bum lag too."

"I's sees ta the ank'll, most likely broke." Ham volunteered.

"Git thet hat an put it back on he's head, Boy. Thet's the best we'ens ken do. We'ens need ta git hem out of the sun. He's eyes look funny"

"I ken put a tight wrap on thet ank'll, Pap; I ken do thet much."

"'Kay, Ham, ya do thet, an Will, ya find hem a crutch ta walk wit."

Ruff was able to keep up with some of the discussion over him but they seemed to be talking so fast and foreign that he couldn't quite follow the strange voices. *It sounded like they were going to try to help him. They must be good people.* Slowly his head cleared and he could see one of the three men standing over him. One man *who looks more like a boy* had his shirt off and was tearing an undershirt into a strip of cloth. Before Ruff realized it the boy started putting a make shift figure eight ankle wrap on his sprain. Soon a third man came into Ruffs view with a tree branch fashioned into a kind of arm crutch. They helped Ruff to his feet. For a minute, Ruff thought he was going to pass out again, but the episode passed and the man with the tree branch placed it under his right armpit. Surprisingly it was just the right height for Ruff to lean on and transfer his weight so he could move his tender left leg. *He could WALK, sort of.*

"I can't thank you fellows enough. You've made my day. Is there anything I can do for you?"

"Naw, we'ens jest out huntin," the young one said, off handedly.

"Hunting? There's no hunting in Roosevelt with a shotgun." Ruff's observation had not missed the shotgun carried by the older man and became puzzled by its presence.

Ruff thought he noticed the old man give the boy a stern look. "He meen we'ens mush'rumin, thet's it, we'ens mush'rumin."

"It's a little late for mushrooms," replied Ruff. "I guess there might be a few still out, but the season is near past."

"Hay, ya figger it out. We'ens best be gitin."

Ruff thought Pap appeared to be getting very nervous. "What's that really for?" Ruff said motioning toward the shotgun.

"Tection," Pap answered with out missing a beat.

"Protection from what?" Ruff shot back.

"Bar an such," Pap responded and with a jerk of his head motioned for the other two to follow him as he started toward the woods on the far side of the grassy clearing. They left Ruff standing alone and never looked back as they disappeared into the woods.

Well, I'll be. Doesn't that beat all? They're traveling through the Roosevelt National Forest and no gear or food that I could see, and with a shotgun. I don't think the rangers would have approved a permit for him to carry a shotgun. I think my friend Bill Waddle would be interested in visiting with those three. I'll have to put a bug in his ear when I get back. If I get back. I'm not out of this yet.

Ruff started across the grassy clearing moving very slowly but at least upright and he became more confident with each stride he took. The tight ankle wrap and the crutch were working just fine.

If Ruff's circumstances been such that he had access to medical assistance he would have been told that his condition was the result of a concussion. A medical practitioner would have explained that the length of time Ruff was unconscious could indicate the severity of the concussion. During the second and third blackout Ruff was in serious medical trouble.

Often under these conditions a person loses the memory of the events preceding the injury. The most memory loss is right after the injury. Full recovery from a concussion is expected although it takes time to regain memory loss. In some cases full recall of events just before the accident is never achieved. The more stress Ruff put on his medical condition the more hazardous it became for him.

At his age he needed to get some rest if he was to overcome the dangers faced from the concussion. But one good thing in his effort to locate his camp, it kept him active and awake. Ruff needed rest but sleep was not something which a doctor would advise him to succumb. If the brain suffered serious damage, the possibility existed that he might not wake up.

Ruff suspected that he might have a bit of a concussion. With several classes under his belt, he had become very familiar with first aid practices in the field. It was just that he wasn't used to treating himself when it came to the use of what he knew about first aid.

Being somewhat aware of his condition, he tried to *"shake it off,"* as he said many times to young campers. He did not know how much time passed while he was out. An hour, a day, or more?

Ruff, not knowing his condition, had been the one who set a plan in motion and now owned the responsibility of that plan. Without quite understanding why, his determination to locate his camp became paramount in his mind.

Ruff brought his mind back to the present, and realized the sun was beginning to set. Recalling that he had started moving at about one in the afternoon when he started moving, and guessing that the sun sat about seven at this time of the year he figured he had been traveling for about six hours. He needed to find a place to spend the night or at least to rest for a few hours. To keep going during the night could be something to consider since he wasn't searching by observing landmarks, he searched by instinct, and that didn't require light.

Fortunately he spotted a large bush that would work as a shelter. He set to work hacking away some of the interior of the bush to make room for him inside. The debris that he removed from the inside, would be used to thicken the outside by shoving them into the bush stem first. When satisfied with the results, he contemplated the idea of starting a fire. Deciding that it was not so cold that a fire would be needed he opted to forgo the fire as it would attract unwarranted attention. Crawling into his close quarters, he settled in for a rest. The quiet of the night interfered with Ruffs intention to remain awake, he dozed off into a peaceful slumber. Sometime in the night he suddenly awoke. Wondered if a noise had awakened him, or if his internal clock had sounded its alarm telling him it's time to go. He opted for the latter and offered, "Well, I'm wide awake and my head and ankle feel much better, let's to move on."

Taking a short pull from the canteen, he noticed the ankle bandage had pulled loose from walking in the brush. He carefully re-wrapped the ankle, and with the help of the tree branch, crawled out of the bush. Standing up he experienced only a slight light-headedness. He believed that his head was healing from whatever damage occurred in injuring himself. Using the makeshift crutch as a walking stick, he proceeded with only a dull pain. Cautious, he started moving through the woods as though he knew the direction of the lost camp.

After what seemed like a couple of hours, he realized that the day was beginning to break. When the light became a little brighter he became aware of familiar landmarks in his surroundings. Thinking to himself, *I have been here before. I know this place. I concealed my pack over there somewhere in the trees near those bushes alongside that large boulder. Yes, there is the marker I set out. I found it, and in the dark too; instinct worked.*

Retrieving his pack, he ravenously ate a cold packet of food and took three more aspirin with a swig of water. In the process he realized that this spot could not be his base camp, the food cache was incomplete. He started talking to himself, "I remember being on the Cache La Poudre tributary with Mike. I don't remember why I left the tributary, but I bet Mike is still there waiting for me to return. I need to fix this ankle and then get to Mike."

After unwrapping his ankle and using some Deep Heat Sport Cream, he massaged his sprain, which now had more colors to it than a rainbow. Shouldering his pack, he again spoke aloud to himself, "now let's see about finding Mike, wherever he is."

CHAPTER 8

Traveling with a sense of purpose, Mike had made good time moving out of the valley where the cabin was located. He could see the shadow of the high ridge in the moonlight that had graciously appeared over the top of the valley wall shortly after he started from the cabin. The night was cool, not cold, and he traveled comfortably. He felt so strong that he decided to climb to the top of the ridge and then determine a southern direction.

Anxiously he pressed on. Mike planned to get as far away from the cabin as time would allow and to travel as noiselessly as possible. His greatest fear was running into the three men from whom he wanted to avoid at all costs. Reaching the ridge, he stopped to rest and take his first drink from the water bottle.

Yuk! The water in the jar tasted awful. Thinking a through rinse of the bottle when it had first been found near the shed would clear it of any harmful bacteria, Mike failed to realized what taste the warm water would take on. Now, wondering just what had been in the bottle, there was nothing to do but hope it would not have a bad effect on his system. With no label on it, the clear jug gave no indication what might have originally been in the container. Deciding that one sip at a time would be the limit for him, he tightened the lid and strung to bottle back on his belt.

After resting for about twenty minutes, he rose and inspected the skyline. There was just a hint of light now from the moon as it started to disappear as it hurried toward the horizon. All that his eyes could really see were trees, and geographically the terrain appeared to him as a large ridge that ran at a ninety-degree angle from the box canyon. As much as his desire wanted to see, nothing appeared to him that would indicate the presence of a river. Knowing only that the trip from where the bear shooting took place, to the cabin, they had not crossed a river or stream of any size. Even at the cabin the source of water consisted of an old hand dug well about 20 feet deep. Mike's experience with the well had told him there was very little water in the well. His experience with the well had been limited to the times when he visited it during the night and the people in the cabin were asleep. When the bucket had been lowered, it seemed to hit the bottom of the well at the same time it hit water.

Believing that the four of them had come along the top of the ridge some distance after ascending it from the south, Mike decided to try to retrace the route they had taken coming into the canyon. After about an hour's walk along the top of the ridge, he found a well-used animal trail leading off the ridge headed more or less in a southern direction. Lacking light, he was concerned that he might lose track of the trail but he remembered what he had heard Ruff say many times and decided it was best to take the animal trail.

It was a steep decline and the trail meandered back and forth taking advantage of angles, thus making it easier to navigate the downward slope of the ridge. He lost his footing at one point and slid about fifteen feet on his backside. Mike knew that carelessness could lead to injury. Pledging himself to be more careful and re-gaining his place on the trail he continued following it down the slope. Only now he stepped with care, for fear that if he became injured his troubles would be deadly serious.

As he worked his way down the slope, Mike tried to remember some of the pointers Ruff told young people in his many lectures to school and church groups. *He always told them that there were a number of things to remember if they ever got lost in the woods: number 1—**Stay put**. The first and most difficult thing is not to panic. Running here and there uses up energy. Also moving around only makes you harder to find by those looking for you. So much for that advice. If I stay put, I end up what, a life-long prisoner or dead? I don't think there is anyone who is looking for me yet. But I can't take a chance that they're not, I've got to keep moving.*

*Number 2—**think**-and remember the rule of three; you can live three minutes without air, three hours without warmth, three days without water, and three weeks without food. I have water and food such as it is, so I'm okay there.*

*Number 3—**observe**—Use your compass and map to locate your position and heading. Look for landmarks to identify on the map, or to orient yourself to head in the right direction. Check how much daylight you have and what the weather is doing. Do you need to find shelter? It would be nice; Ruff, but right now I need to put some distance between the people in that cabin and* *me. I don't have a map, and right now I don't have daylight. The weather is fine though, thanks for asking. By the way, Ruff, why don't I have a map? Why didn't you leave one at the camp when you decided to leave me?*

Ruff's fourth thing to remember was **prepare**—*Plan your stay, tell someone where you are going, build a fire or shelter. Gather plenty of tinder, and wood. Yeah, right, Ruff! I can't do any of those things. It's not like I planned this, and you weren't there to tell anything to. I don't need a shelter, at least not now, and if I did build a fire I might attract the very people that I am trying to get away from. Good advice, Ruff.*

Mike was so engrossed in his thoughts that he hadn't paid attention to the loose rocks on the animal trail. His foot slid on the poor footing and he tumbled off the path into a sticky bush. He put out his arm to catch himself and his hand came down on a branch of the bush right on some stickers. "Ouch!" The verbal response was automatic and the word came out of his mouth before he realized it. His own voice surprised him, and he froze. Cautiously he looked around as if someone might be watching. He inspected the terrain for any movement. No one appeared.

He next examined his hand and found several places where it had been pricked, but no stickers. *Thanks, Ruff, why don't you say something about watching where you're going?*

With effort he pulled himself up. Feeling a sting, he once again examined his hand for stickers. Not finding any, he dusted the dirt off his arm and pant legs. Noticing that the sky was getting lighter and his surroundings were easier to see, he thought about his situation.

It's near daybreak. That means a whole different ballgame. Now I have to worry about someone coming after me. I wonder if Pap and the boys have left the cabin. Did they check on me before leaving? If so, what will they do? Will they start out after me? No, they would be anxious to get on with their hunting. Besides, they didn't seem to be very concerned about me while in their custody anyway. Don't kid yourself Mike, they wouldn't want you telling some ranger about their shooting the cub bears, and probably not about them homesteading in a National Forest either.

*   *   *

Mike left the animal trail he had been following for the last several hours when it entered one of the many grassy clearings that dotted the landscape in the valleys of the national forest. *I can't afford to move through an open space like that,* he thought to himself. *If the three from the cabin were looking for me, I would be easy to spot. I will have to stay under the cover of the woods and go around the open meadow. Besides, I'm starting to get hungry, I need to stop and rest a little anyway.* Mike soon found an area that offered him some protection from being seen. There was a clump of bushes between several trees that formed an ally way. It would hide him from being sighted by anyone coming down the valley floor. Mike made himself a small nest-like area between some of the bushes. Reaching into the food sock that was tied onto his belt, he pulled out a chunk of turnip. *I will try this first, to see if it is fit to eat,* he mused, *if it tastes okay then I can try a piece of the meat.* After ingesting three chunks of turnip and two pieces of meat, he leaned back on his elbow and contemplated his next move. He was so lost in his thoughts that at first he didn't consciously become aware of the movement of one of the bushes. But when they moved the second time he froze with fear. Something was coming through the bushes. *Someone is coming toward me.*

CHAPTER 9

Ruff had been traveling for several hours. He was now moving down stream of the Cache La Poudre tributary, toward the location of the campsite he had picked for his outing with Mike. During the travel time, the headache Ruff had been suffering from, had subsided considerably. Also the walking stick had been discarded for a smaller cane-like one. He attributed the improvement of his well being as much to the additional three aspirin that had been taken as to the passage of time. As the headache disappeared, his memory improved. Though still unable to recall what he was doing before awaking to the head injury, he could now put some of the pieces of the puzzle in his mind together. He recalled that the two of them had been camping on the Cache La Poudre tributary and that he had left for some reason. Some unknown force was now pulling him back to that camp.

As he seemed to be constantly thirsty since the encounter with the three men who assisted him on the trail, Ruff was thankful for the presence of the mountain stream, and the water purification tablets in his pack. As he wondered if the thirst was related to the knot on his head, his mind returned to thoughts about the three men. *Their speech did not sound like any that he had heard in this part of the country. It sounded more like the two fellows in his infantry squad when he was in the army. They were from somewhere in West Virginia if he remembered correctly. That's a long way from Denver,* Ruff thought to himself. *I wonder how they came to be in Roosevelt? They didn't seem to be in any hurry, and they were traveling light. Only one had a pack and it was more like a knapsack. Maybe they had a camp near the grassy clearing where I met them.*

Reaching the campsite along the mountain stream, Disappointed in not finding Mike at the camp, Ruff made a thorough search. Hoping to find something that would tell him where Mike could have gone or if he would be coming back any time soon. There were several things that quickly became obvious to him. One, the food pack was still hung securely high off the ground. The tent looked like it had not been used. Mike's sleeping bag and ground cloth were swinging from a rope stretched between two trees. Mike's personal pack was missing, and also his hunting knife. From remnants Ruff found inside the fire ring, he could tell that Mike had eaten several packets of food. Also in the fire site there were several rather large log ends, and a substantial supply of wood near the fireplace. Mike apparently had a very large fire going shortly before he left. Ruff also found a stew container that had been severely chewed on. It appeared to Ruff that Mike had every intention of returning.

In answer to a question that formed in his mind, Ruff decided that Mike had been gone for several days: how many was difficult to determine as there had been a shower or two of rain since the fire had gone out. What concerned Ruff was that it appeared that Mike had taken very little food with him and that the water purification packets were still secure in the food pack. Without food and water, Mike would be in trouble after several days, maybe a week or more. *The weather has been mild, so he should be fine in that respect. But if he is injured or lost, he's in trouble, because I have no idea which direction he may have gone.*

Ruff reluctantly decided that the best thing for him to do would be to stay at the camp and nurse his sore ankle. And hope that Mike would soon return. An uneasy feeling began to gnaw at his insides. If anything happened to Mike, Jennifer would disown him. Not wanting to process the thoughts starting in his mind, Ruff set about to reorganize the camp and wait impatiently for Mike's return.

CHAPTER 10

When the black bear came into view, Mike almost fainted. It looked huge, and Mike didn't move a muscle. He was in full view of the bear with his back against a large boulder. *Do bears have good eyesight?* Mike wondered. *Maybe it helps that my clothes are about the same color as the rock I'm up against.* The bear was about ten yards away from him and was feeding on some of the dried berries still on the bushes left over from last year's crop. Because of the way the animal was behaving, Mike didn't think it was all that interested in the berries. It seemed to be preoccupied with checking the area, expecting to see something. Suddenly the bear raised its nose to the air and sniffed. *She smells something, or is searching for something.* Mike became engrossed in watching the bear's behavior. She went back to feeding. *Isn't it strange?* He thought, *She seems to be concerned about what is around her. As if she is in strange territory. Or maybe she knows I'm here!* Then Mike noticed something: the bear was limping on its left front paw. *That's the she-bear. The one from my camp. What is she doing here?* Mike then realized he didn't know where "here" was. *If this is the same bear that visited the campsite, then how far can it be? How far does a bear roam? Does this bear have a territory that it stays in or does she just keep moving forever across the country?*

Mike suddenly realized that he already knew part of the answers to his own questions. He was reminded of a time in one of his social pathology classes when a professor was trying to make a point on something about human behavior. *Mike recalled a study the instructor mentioned to the class on bear behavior and its comparison to human behavior. We were assigned a book to read by Benjamin Kilham, called Among the Bears. I found it quite interesting. The first thing the author wanted his readers to realize was that bears are animals and so are humans. That they are similar in their reactions to certain stimuli.*

Kilham stated in his book that female bears have a core home range which they share with their off spring. But if food becomes scarce the female will roam outside the home range and enter another bear's territory. Kilham went on to say that the reaction of the second bear depended on the quality and quantity of food in the second territory. I'll bet that's her problem, she's either looking for her cubs or she is out of her territory and is concerned about it, Mike thought.

So I still don't know how far this mother bear has roamed from the campsite. But, at least, I must be headed in the right direction. The bear seemed content to munch on the berries, and Mike was content to sit and watch. Observing the bear, Mike searched his memory to remember more about what Kilham had written on bear behavior.

Ruff has probably never read a book and he seems to know a lot about bears. I know he has had several encounters with them. But this guy Kilham had raised bear cubs that were orphans. He knew about them also. This brought to mind what Kilham had written about meeting a bear on the trail and he had to admit that it was pretty much the same as what Ruff had told him the first night of the campout, except Kilham was comparing it to human behavior.

Mike was able to bring to mind what Kilham wrote about bear behavior when they meet humans. His first encounter, like Mike's was with a female bear.

At first the bear showed aggression by charging several times. Each time Kilham stood his ground and hollered at the bear and she backed off and waited. "She was doing the same thing I was doing." He wrote. "I was observing her and she was observing me."

Bears, he wrote, *read body language and sounds much better than we do. Inflections and expressions in our words give much more information than people realize. Your actions, when encountering a bear are to show that you are neither a weakling nor a threat to it. Bears have a social make up based on dominance. The only bear to fear is one that won't run from you, or leave. Bears also have a strong sense of personal space. The distance or area of personal space at which they won't back down, varies from bear to bear. If the bear does the jaw popping, huffing, earth stomping, or false charging routine, then you are inside the personal space of that bear.*

Mike surprised himself on how much of the book he remembered. *Ruff would say, "I told you all of that and you didn't have to read a book to hear it."* Mike grinned to himself, *Ruff defending his own personal space!*

Mike suddenly realized that the bear was no longer at the berries. *Where did she go?* Mike asked himself, *she was just here a minute ago. Now what do I do? I don't want to start walking and walk right into her. Now I have to go into a "wait and see" mode.*

CHAPTER 11

Ruff busied himself around the campsite. He wasn't satisfied with his decision to sit and wait. No, Ruff wasn't satisfied, *but what else could he do? Where could he look? He had no idea in which direction Mike might have gone. He had no choice except to wait and hope for the best.* Would Mike come back?

Looking for things to do, Ruff decided to relocate the fire pit back to its original location, the one chosen before Mike had changed it. Ruff's thoughts opened up, *from what I could tell through the binoculars Mike changed it because of the rainstorm. It must have flooded out on him. I purposely located it in this low spot so it would have a good updraft. But I can see why Mike moved it.* Ruff recalled the events of that morning. *Hey! I'm beginning to remember things that happened that day I injured my head and foot. My head must be healing as well as my ankle.*

Examining the spit upright stakes that hold the spit across the blaze of the fire, Ruff pulled his hands back in his surprise. *Whoa, I don't remember seeing this, Mike must have had to re-do the spit supports also. This isn't my work; I didn't make this spit. But I have to admit it's good work. And he did a good job of finding green wood for the spit so it wouldn't burn on him. The boy's got possibilities; he'll make a frontiersman yet!*

Suddenly, Ruff felt a presence. He looked up; the three stood not twenty feet from him. *Dang, I must be getting old, how could I have been so engrossed in my own thoughts that I missed feeling their presence long before they got this close?* He did not consider the fact that it was mid afternoon, that the sun was now directly behind the three, as an excuse for his negligence. It would have been difficult for Ruff to see anyone approaching from that direction. But Ruff knew excuses didn't count for anything when you are in the wilderness. A bad feeling came over him about their return to his space. *Why are they here when Roosevelt is such a big place? There is so much space around for them to use that it is unreal they need to be in this place.*

Ruff looked at the three men he had met earlier on the trail. He had appreciation for their help in getting him on his feet, but there was something about them that bothered him. And the shotgun that the oldest carried didn't help him lose his concern.

"You boys lost?" Ruff asked, knowing that he didn't really care what the answer would be. As it turned out, they didn't answer his question at all.

"We'ens wonderin 'ear ya fixin ta lite thet fire up?"

"No, I hadn't planned on it right now; I was just fixing it so it would be ready when time comes for the evening meal."

"We'ens could use some coffee, Ya make some coffee fer ya guests." Ruff wasn't sure if that was a question or a statement.

"I don't have much coffee; I usually drink green tea." Ruff stretched the truth a little bit here, but he did drink green tea on occasion. He just didn't like being told what to do, particularly by these three.

"We'ens would a'preate the 'ostality, we'ens would. We'ens been wit out drenk all day. We'ens could use a drenk of coffee. Thet'ed be mity neig'borly of ya."

And with that the old man, quicker on his feet than Ruff thought he would be, covered the twenty feet and plopped down next to the newly reconstructed fire ring. Only when Ruff made no attempt to challenge the old man, or to object to his presence, did his two sons follow him to the fire ring. Ruff wished there were some way of telling whether or not the shotgun was loaded, but he knew the only way would be if someone popped the breach. Ruff also knew that the old man was too wiley to fall for any ruse to get that to happen, so he had to assume that the gun was loaded.

Ruff decided that under the circumstances it would be best for him to oblige the three and began to kindle the fire pit. Making a fire didn't take Ruff long and he soon had a blaze going. He put a pot of water on the spit, and leaned back. He knew it would take some time for the water to heat.

He needed time to study the situation and determine just what the three were up to. What did they want from Ruff? Surely they wanted something more than coffee. But for the life of him he couldn't figure them out. Ruff guessed that he would have plenty of time to find out. They didn't seem to be in any hurry to make something happen.

"How about I fix you boys some green tea? That would hit the spot, wouldn't it? Some nice hot green tea." Ruff's grin looked a lot like a smirk.

"Jest some coffee weel be fen." Pap wasn't biting.

"You sure? Green tea is mighty tasty." Ruff believed in pushing back when pushed besides the situation irritated him.

"I's sad coffee, an thet's thet." Pap shifted the shotgun in his lap.

Ruff decided that if he were going to have to serve the three coffee then it would be instant coffee and like it or not, they would not complain. Not if they wanted a second cup.

As Ruff poured hot water into the three cups for the second time, he had begun to realize that he had become their prisoner and they were his keepers. No one said a thing; the three were enjoying their drink with great gusto. The slurping and belching normally would not have gained much attention around a campfire, however, Ruff thought it to be contrived and a bit much. Ruff could not resist the temptation of letting them know he wasn't intimidated.

"You boys make a lot of noise when you drink coffee. It's a good thing I didn't serve you green tea. When you drink tea you have to sip quietly and hold your little pinky just so." Ruff, with an exaggerated grin on his face demonstrated with his little finger curled perfectly.

The faces of the two younger men took on a menacing look. They knew that they were being made fun of and weren't taking it very well, all to the delight of Ruff. The old man's somber face, however, never changed expression, not even to glance in Ruff's direction.

"Well, I reckon you fellows are in a hurry to get back to your camp before dark." Ruff knew this was called "testing the waters." No one responded.

Instead, without taking his eyes off Ruff, the old man pointed the shotgun in the direction of the food pack hanging by a rope high in the air. The older son, Will, got up, walked over to where the rope was tied to a tree and with one swift motion, pulled his hunting knife from his belt and sliced through the rope. The pack landed on the ground with a heavy thud.

"Look like it mite be heavy wit food." The old man made it sound like he had just discovered a gold mine, thought Ruff. "Brang thet thing over 'ear son, I's mite be gitin hongree. Let's sees wot we'ens got ta eat."

Ruff felt that he should at least try to defend his territory. He started to stand up. Quick as a fox, the old man swung the shotgun in his direction and snapped back the triggers of both barrels of the gun. Ruff hearing the click, click, froze.

"Jest sat back boy, thes don't corn'cern ya enny. We'ens jest wonderin bout somptin ta eat."

Ruff immediately returned his body to the ground. "I wanted to just try and help the boy; he didn't need to cut my new rope." Ruff's anger had gone beyond testing, on the inside he fumed, and it showed.

The youngest of the three sat quietly just far enough from the fire light so that Ruff could not make out the features of his face. He had his left hand placed on the handle of a large hunting knife secured in a sheath attached to his belt.

The old man released the triggers of both barrels of the shotgun and laid it in his lap. He and his older son rifled through the pack with slow meticulous precision. Once during the process the old man made a comment to his son about how well prepared Ruff appeared to be and how efficiently he packed for living in the woods. He concluded with, "Ya do a good job of packin fer a week ender."

Ruff was not impressed with the compliment and pushed his territorial challenge a bit further. "I did have that tightly packed and organized in the order of which items I would probably use first, but your grubby hands have laid waste to that. I could have told you what the pack contained and saved you the task of having to check it out. Better yet, you could have just left it alone."

The old man gave him a hard look, then softened it somewhat and asked, "wot ya mean wit thet word grubby, boy. Wot ya mean wit thet?"

He shifted the shotgun in his lap so that the muzzle of the gun pointed directly at Ruff. Ruff understood that the old man wasn't into playing the game of "testing."

Ruff wasn't through with his defense though, "That *is* my pack; it's not polite to rummage through another man's belongings without permission."

The old man's face turned hard again. "An it ain't po'ite not ta offer a man a bite ta et on the trail. Now why don't ya jest heat up three of these packages of beef stew or wot 'ear it be, an do it qick'ly and quietly."

With that he tossed Ruff three packets of food, and motioned toward the fire. Deciding that testing time had ended, and being out gunned and out manned. This would be a poor time to make a stand against these three. Adding a little more water to the pot on the spit, he placed the packets in the steaming liquid.

CHAPTER 12

Mike shifted his position against the boulder. The sun high in the sky and anxious to get back on the trail; Mike worried himself about doing so. He didn't know where the old sow had disappeared to and had no idea if the old man and his two sons were on his trail or not. Plus being a little antsy about staying in one spot for very long, because it seemed to be best, in his mind, to move often and as far from the cabin as possible. In his head he heard the "get a move on," as Ruff so frequently told him.

Knowing he had to move sooner or later, he checked the meager gear he possessed, and being satisfied that everything was in place, stood and determined a direction. The high ridge that had traversed during the night had already played out. Needing to find somewhere to replenish his water supply, Mike decided to continue moving south. He knew that in his decision-making he had selected south, mostly because that direction was still down hill and easier to travel and that would be the logical place to find a water source.

The going got a lot easier and Mike made good time moving through the sparsely wooded area of the valley floor. Occasionally checking his little compass to reassure himself of his belief in pursuing a southerly direction. As he hiked along another animal trail, Mike began glancing at the sun. Remembering that Ruff could tell the time of day from the sun, an internal determination, something he was not aware he possessed, convinced him that he could do the same. Recalling that Ruff said when the sun shone from directly over head the time was 12:00 noon, so now he decided, it must be early afternoon. The sun had reached its apex and had drifted toward the west about ten degrees. *2: o'clock,* Mike thought, *time for a break.*

Looking around and taking in his surroundings, he spotted a good "hiding" place, one that would offer protection from being seen by anyone moving along the trail. Mike realized that he didn't know which to be more worried about: someone coming along from behind where he had just came from, or running into someone coming toward him from where he was going. *What a dilemma, I am afraid of meeting someone and at the same time I need someone to tell me where I am.*

Suddenly it dawned on him, *there has to be other hikers in these woods. Ruff says Roosevelt is a very popular place for wilderness campers and back trail hikers. Surely, I am not the only one in these woods. I should come across other hikers. But with my luck I'll run into those guys from the cabin, then what? What would they do? Would they take me back to the cabin? Why would they do that? Or would they decide I was more trouble than I was worth and—?* Shaking his head at his thoughts, Mike found a spot he liked and settled down to rest.

Mike had been traveling most of the night and all of the morning. Once he stopped and settled into a comfortable spot, he succumbed to his exhaustion. When he jerked awake, the first thing he did was to notice the position of the sun. *It has traveled from overhead as much, or more than when I stopped. I have slept for over two hours. It must be about four in the afternoon, maybe later.* Before getting to his feet, Mike took a look around and gave himself a chance to study the surrounding terrain.

Taking a long drink from his water jar, which still had a funny taste about it, he decided not to eat any of his food. Rising and checking his compass once again, off he started in a southern direction.

He had traveled less than an hour when the sound came—the unmistakable sound of running water. He had found it, the little stream where his campsite was located. He was safe. Ruff would be there and they could go home. Everything would be back to normal.

Mike moved quickly in the direction of the sound of the water. When he caught site of the stream he was elated. Then it struck him, *do I go upstream or down?* Down, definitely down stream, because I must still be far from the campsite.

Deciding that the first thing he needed to do was replenish the meager water supply he carried, Mike knelt down and started refilling the jar. *Wait a minute, I should have some water purification tablets to put in this. Ruff says always—but Ruff isn't here, and Ruff doesn't have to worry about getting thirsty. Still—what if this water is contaminated.*

"If you must use unpurified water for drinking purposes, boil it first." That is what he would tell me, thought Mike. *Straight from the horses mouth.*

To boil water I need a fire. Do I dare start one and maybe attract attention from the men from the cabin? I'll just have to take that chance, 'cause I need some fresh water. Now how do I start the fire, I have no matches. Then he had an idea. Looking around he found some dry tender from the inside of a piece of tree bark. Very carefully he shredded it and using other pieces of bark, created a windbreak to protect his fire when it started. Using the magnifying glass on his compass he aimed the sun's rays on the tender. At first he had trouble keeping the glass aimed at one spot of the tender, but soon a small whiff of smoke drifted up from it.

As the smoke became more denser, he gently blew on the tender and magically a little flame erupted. He quickly added some more tender and then graduated to small pieces of wood. Soon he had a good blaze going. Suddenly, a gust of wind reminded him of more of Ruffs' lecture. *Remember that you must have a stone or earthen barrier around your campfire in a national forest.* Mike quickly collected an armload of rocks from near the stream. After fashioning a double layer of rock around the fire, he sat back and admired his handiwork.

Proud of what he had accomplished, he set about creating a spit over the fire. Only after having it nearly complete did he realize that one thing was missing. He had no pot.

Returning to the creek, he searched along the shore for something he could use. Then he spotted it. At first he thought it was a tin can, but as he dug into the sandy shore, he realized that what he had found was an old miner's pan for separating gold from other rock. He checked to see if it would still hold water. There were a couple of rust spots along the bottom outside ring but no holes. He washed it out as best he could and headed back to his little fire. Rigging a second spit across the fire he now had a platform to place the pan above the fire. Using his jar to carry water, he filled the pan about half full. Adding a couple of short chunks of wood to the fire pit, he sat back and waited for the water to heat.

As he watched the water, it suddenly dawned on him that he could heat up some of the pieces of meat and turnip, if he had something to hold them in the water. Dismissing the idea of using his old sock, and once again going to the creek, he searched anew. Finding several pieces of plastic before coming across a small tin container which Mike thought it must have been an old sardine tin. *Thanks for those campers who didn't hear Ruffs' "leave it as you found it," campaign.* Mike knew his personal supplies had just added the pan and tin can to what he had to carry out of the forest.

Having eaten, and with a full jar of water, Mike was once again ready to continue his journey. *I still believe that I must go down stream. I'm not past the camp yet; I haven't traveled far enough.* Carefully Mike began picking his way along the creek. As he hiked along, he kept a sharp eye out for signs of man or animal. *I don't know which I would rather find, the men or the bear.* Ideally, he finally realized the correct answer would be neither, *I guess.*

Mike suddenly stumbled over a log half buried in the sand and rock along the creek. "Ouch!" He exclaimed. "I didn't see that." When he looked around to see if anyone had heard him, he became aware of the fact that the sun had set and darkness was approaching. *The sun has already set,* he thought. *And it's getting cool; I need to find some place to hole up for the night. Some place where I can stay warm, maybe a clump of boulders, or bushes to use as a windbreak.*

He began looking a little further away from the creek bed for a good spot to spend the night. Finally after some time he came across an indentation along a rock ledge and decided that he would have to make do with that for protection. Using his hunting knife he fashioned a shelter out of bush branches and tree limbs found on the ground, leaving a hole just big enough to crawl into. It fit perfectly. As soon as the comfortable "nest" warmed, sleep came peacefully.

CHAPTER 13

Upon awakening early the next morning, Mike felt refreshed. There was plenty of light to see by, but as of yet, the sun had not risen. Watching a pair of cottontail rabbits, he suddenly remembered something Ruff had included in one of his lectures. *Watch what animals eat. If it is good for them, then it is probably safe for you to eat.*

Mike crawled out of his makeshift shelter and moved to where the rabbits were eating. He cautiously picked some of the plant shoots and gingerly tasted one leaf. It didn't seem to have much taste, but to Mike, at least it wasn't bitter. He decided to pick a handful and save them for later. *They will go well with a chunk of meat. That will stretch my food supply.* As an afterthought, he also used his hunting knife and dug up some of the roots of the plant. *I can test these out later also. If they don't make me sick, I can use them for food also.*

Mike took a glance back at the shelter he had made for the night, and with a sigh, turned and started toward the stream. Stopping abruptly, he turned once again in the direction of the shelter. Retracing his steps, he began to demolish the shelter,—*just in case someone comes along that isn't friendly; I don't want them to know I was here.*

After sweeping the entire area with a tree branch, Mike was satisfied that all trace of his having been there had been removed. He moved once again in the direction of the mountain stream and followed it as it rushed down hill toward—*toward what?* Thought Mike. *Toward good or evil? Toward safety or danger?* Mike shook his head, *I guess it's as Ruff would say, "Sometimes you just have to trust your instincts, and take what comes your way."*

Mike made good time for the first hour or so, but then the stream ran through an area that was thick with brambles that had good-sized thorns on them. In addition, they seemed to grow right up to the water edge. Mike was forced to wade the creek for a time. The water wasn't very deep, but the rocky bottom was so sharp and uneven that Mike had to slow down and take care of his footing. He didn't want to stumble and end up all wet. After passing the bramble patch, he noticed that the sun was well into the morning sky and he started looking for a spot to build a fire. He was famished and wanted to try out his newly found food supply. He soon located a place to build his fire, it butted up against a stone ledge and somewhat away from the creek. He didn't want to be surprised by someone who might also be traveling the creek.

Once again, he meticulously prepared some tinder and used the magnifying glass. Mike soon had a small fire going, and using the miners' pan he carried stuffed in his shirt, started heating water. Green vegetables were not Mike's favorite food but when he tasted the hot mixture of greens, peeled, diced roots, with some of his bear meat and potatoes, in a little boiled water, he was impressed with himself. *I should be a "living in the wild" chef,* he proudly thought.

Mike leaned back against the ledge thinking, *I wonder if I truly am on the right track. Is this the same stream as my campsite, or am I still lost? What if I follow this stream and never spot anything that looks familiar? What do I do if I run into the three from the cabin? What about running into another bear? I have a lot of questions and no answers. And the biggest question of all: What happened to Ruff? Why did he leave camp? Did he leave of his own accord, or did he run into some one that did him harm? Why would he just go off and leave me? Well, I can answer that one, he wouldn't. Would he? No! He knows how Mom would react. She would chew him out something terrible, disown him and then ground him for life. So what happened? Is he at the campsite waiting for me? If so, how long will he wait? I bet he would beat it back to the ranger's office, that guy, that friend of his, and organize a search party. What if there is a whole bunch of people out there some where looking for me right now? What if I built a huge fire so it could be seen from a long distance and got their attention? What if I helped myself by being found by—by whom? By those three from the cabin? What if I attracted their attention? What if they found me? What would they do?*

As Mike lost himself in his thoughts he fell asleep. In his dream he floated down a river all alone on a raft. Swimming beside the raft was Ruff with a wide grin on his face as he watched the three men in a canoe, paddling after Mike and coming ever so closer as the heavy raft slowly floated with the current. *Ruff, why don't you help me?* Mike called out. The attempt at sleep was fretful. His late morning nap didn't last long. He was soon wide awake. *I slept through noon: I need to get going.*

CHAPTER 14

Ruff decided he would never make a good prisoner; not only did he detest the tightness of the rope, but he also disliked the whole idea of someone restricting his freedom of movement. The three men had finished their meal, without offering any to Ruff. Fearing that Ruff might make an escape during the night, at the order of the old man, the youngest member of the trio gleefully proceeded to hobble Ruff as if he were a common horse. A nag that might decide the grazing was better somewhere else and disappear into the dark of the night.

"We'ens dont want ya ta be won'derin way in the nite," The old man said. "Nor do we'ens want ya ta be causin anny trouble, nor risin a ruckus an causin some one ta 'vistagate. We'ens ken take care of 'ear own self. We'ens don't need outsiders ta be messin in 'ear bizz'nes. Ya git me, boy?"

Ruff didn't answer the question and the old man didn't expect him to; they both knew that to understand the meaning of Pap's words was a fact, it wasn't a choice. Ruff had made no comment as Ham worked at trussing him up. It was now completely dark, as the moon would not appear until later in the night, and Ruff could tell from the sounds coming from the three men that all were asleep. How deeply they slept, he wasn't so sure. He knew that the old man was not to be trusted. And was probably a light sleeper or at least a mean spirited one if awakened before his sleep was finished.

Testing the ropes around his legs, Ruff found that the two boys knew how to tie knots and their technique for hobbling was equally as good. Ruff worked diligently on the ropes. And eventually they loosened. After about an hour, he was rewarded for his efforts when the ropes fell free enough that he could slip one foot out of the bonds. In no time, the other foot was also free, and Ruff began to military crawl out of the area. His route took him around the fire site and within inches of the three still snoring with gusto.

Ruff thought as soundly as those guys sleep I could be a one-man marching band with a full percussion section and I would not have been heard. Quietly, he collected some of his belongings from the ground around the rifled packs he and Mike had carried into the campsite. Besides grabbing some personal items that he knew would be lost if left behind, he also collected several packets of food and in the little light available, other survival equipment, he could carry with him. He was able to find one ground cloth he could use as a sleeping bag, and two small pots to be used on a fire pit. His knapsack was full and Ruff knew that to try to leave with any more supplies would mean re-packing the big camp pack and that would just slow him down. Besides, he had enough to survive in the woods as it was, he didn't need much and traveling light means traveling fast.

Slipping quietly out of the camp, Ruff headed upstream of the little tributary of the Cache La Poudre River. His plan was to hike out of the lowlands to the Canyon Lakes District Office, located on a high ridge above the river itself. Once there, he could enlist the aid of his pal Bill Waddle. Bill in return could alert the Ranger Division located at the Park headquarters. They would make short work of the three renegades who had virtually kidnapped him.

Ruff figured it would be a hike of at least four hours during the day. Hiking at night would increase that three-fold, so his plan was to follow the stream and put some distance between himself and the camp, then wait for daybreak to take a more direct route toward Bill's office. He anticipated that the three would not realize he was gone until they woke in the morning By then he would leave the stream and head through the woods where his chances of being spotted were slim.

As the new day's light filtered through the early morning haze, Ruff believed that he had traveled about six miles up stream from the campsite. He traversed some rough terrain and at one point was slowed down by a collection of downed trees that blocked his side of the stream. Because of the high rock ledge that lined much of his side of the little tributary, he was forced to cross the creek and make his way up the other side, all before re-crossing the creek again and continuing on his way.

Now as the morning broke, he was feeling the cold from the dampness of his trousers legs and wished he could stop and build a fire to dry out. But he knew that was out of the question as it was necessary to continue to put some distance between him and the three men who were by this time undoubtedly pursuing him. *Or would they hi-tail it out of the park?* Ruff figured the three would more likely seek revenge over flight. They didn't seem to be the type to run from a threat. No matter what, his first priority was to reach Bill's office and get the Rangers on their trail. He knew that Bill ran a tight ship and would never tolerate any camper abusing the park or anyone or anything in it.

Besides, making a threat with a shotgun was a crime in or out of the boundaries of the park. In addition to that, the Rangers would be interested in hearing what the three were doing in a National Forest with a shotgun in the first place. They certainly weren't looking for mushrooms as the old man had said. My guess is that when the youngest lad had answered Ruff's question with "huntin" he was referring to something besides mushrooms. You don't need a shotgun to hunt mushrooms.

Ruff suddenly realized that he had another problem to present to his good buddy. At Ruff's insistence, Bill would need to organize a search party to locate Mike. *Where could that boy be?* Shaking his head, Ruff thought about the last time he remembered seeing Mike.

If my memory is correct, the last I saw of Mike was when he had just chased an old sow bear out of the campsite. She had a slight limp and two cubs with her that were probably a little under 2 years old. Mike had been lucky that she was a camp bear and didn't take him as a threat to her cubs. Camp bears are used to humans and usually don't challenge a human unless there is food or cubs involved. But how long ago did this happen? How did Mike get away from the campsite without my knowing it?

What will Bill think when he asks me these questions and I tell him, "I don't know."

Focusing on the present, Ruff picked a direction into the woods. Leaving the little creek behind bothered him, as it was the only connection with Mike that he had. He also knew that the creek was the only landmark that would be of any value for Mike to find his way in the wilderness of Roosevelt. But Ruff also realized that it was paramount for him to seek assistance in his search for Mike. *What if Mike ran into those three? If they decided he was somehow a threat to them, what would they do? What wouldn't they do? Mike against the three of them? He wouldn't stand a chance.*

Ruff shook his head at the thought and trudged on into the woods. *I have another twelve miles to cover and a high ridge to climb. It will take me most of the day to reach the district office and Bill Waddle.*

CHAPTER 15

The sun was just making its way into the western sky when Mike awoke. *I slept through noon; I need to get going.* Destroying the evidence of his fire and brushing out his footprints around the ledge, so as to leave no trace of his having been there, Mike set out down the creek once again. After traveling for an hour or so, Mike began having trouble staying with the stream. For the past half-hour or so, a high rock ledge hampered his ability to follow the creek. Then he ran into a collection of several downed trees that barricaded his path right up to the bank of the stream. Not seeing any other choice he waded into the stream to cross to the other side.

As he stepped out of the water on the far side of the creek, he carefully selected his steps and watched his footing. It was then that he noticed the impression in the soft sand. Only one boot mark, but there it was as clear as day. Some one had traveled this same route. The imprint was dry and appeared to have been made only hours ago.

I would guess it was made this morning, Mike thought to himself. *And some one going in the opposite direction, from the looks of things. I wonder if it is anybody that I know. It could be one of the three from the cabin or it could be Ruff. That's the only people I know in the park. Of course it could be some other camper or a day hiker, but one thing is sure, I am not alone.*

The fact that other people could be just in front or behind him made Mike a little more aware of his surroundings. Consciously listening for sounds a little more carefully, and searching the terrain around him with more scrutiny. Stay on "full alert," as Ruff would say. "When you sense trouble or danger, trust your instincts and go to full alert." Mike was extra careful as he re-crossed the stream to the other side, and was glad to notice that the rock ledge had disappeared and a patch of woods had taken its place. Now the terrain was much easier to traverse. Also being mindful of the fact that there was only a slight wind and it came from his right needed to be noted. And listening to the amount of noise they made needed to be noted. Ruff's instructions in one of his many lectures, would contain the caution,

"When you are tracking an animal or another person, scent and sound are definite give-a-ways to the adversary that you are on its trail. Keep the wind to your face and make as little noise as possible." Mike still recalling Ruff's lecture continued with his senses tuned to a higher level.

He had barely made fifty yards down stream when he heard the sound. Without understanding how he knew, he acquainted the sound with that of a human voice. A gruff human voice. A voice he had heard before.

Quickly and silently he slid into the woods on his left and hid himself behind a large pine tree. Mike squatted down, and at almost the same time three figures came into view, not fifty feet from him. He noticed that Ham, the youngest of the three, stayed well back from the other two. *That's strange, he thought, why is he not with the other two?*

"Dad nabit, don't ya 'ear boy, why do I's al'ways haft ta repeat my self."

"Pap, ya bean rapeatin yaself ever since we'ens left thet camp." Will had either disappointed Pap or he tried to defend his little brother.

"Don't git smart wit me, boy, I's give ya one cross the chops, ya git smart." Pap hesitated, apparently to see if Will tried to push the issue any further. When Will remained silent, Pap continued his rant.

"Now ya jest quit ya whinnin like a babe and lissen ta me.

"I's jest sez . . ." Ham had crossed Pap, that much was clear to Mike.

"I's know wot ya sed. Now ya lis'en ta wot I's say. I's thot I's taught ya better of knot tyin then wot I's sees wit my own eyes. Thet knot ya tie would not holt a colt, ne'er mind a horse, an ya speck it ta holt a man?"

Now Mike thought he understood why Ham was hanging back. Maybe he was doing his best to avoid the wrath of his father. Although a good fifty feet away from the old man and his two sons, Mike had no problem hearing them, they were quite loud in their speaking. . Mike could hear alright, but was having difficulty following their discussion. He remembered trying to follow the elder sons' dialect at the cabin. He rarely could get all the words spoken by the son. *And that was when he was talking directly to me, Mike mused. What part of the country are these guys from?* He was so intrigued by the three that he forgot that they posed a threat to him. He wanted to examine them as others had studied unusual groups. This is what those reports were all about; this is the real thing.

Recalling studies he read about in books and discussed in the classroom, he realized he could learn from the group right in front of him. *I wanted to study human behavior and social pathology, well believe it or not, I think I found it right here. I must be careful, if they detect me . . .*

"But Pap, ya did'dent sez tie his hands. So's I's . . ."

"I's not wot I's sed an wot I's did'dent sed, now ya lis'en ta me. We'ens got ta find thet feelow wot got away an we'ens weel fix he's wagon, ya 'ear, boys? Now scatter out an find a trace of 'ear he's at. Now scatter!"

The two sons obeyed immediately. Will took one side of the stream and Ham the other. They had their heads down and were intently studying the ground, moving slowly back and forth in a zigzag motion.

Mike watched as the old man kept looking up and down the creek bed and occasionally threw a stern eye at the boys. Mike was puzzled. *What is going on? The boys were carefully searching for signs of something; I wonder what, or who, they are looking for?*

"Pap, thet feelow must bean some ken of ma'ic man. He's left no sign of hizzelf." Will had his hat off and was scratching his unruly and quite long, mop of hair.

"Weel, we'ens weel go upstream ways an keep a sharp look out fer sign. Pap moved toward the stream and motioned to the boys with the shotgun he was carrying. Mike decided to follow at a safe distance. He had to find out what the three were up to and he wanted to observe them without their knowledge. He tried to be as stealthily as possible in his movements. At first, he was successful, as he had the woods to protect him from sight. But then as they approached the rock ledge and fallen trees, he became aware that it was almost impossible to follow without being sighted. At about that time Ham called out.

"Pap, you best take look et thes. I's done found sign."

Pap moved in for a look as Will hung back. Mike noticed Will's actions. *That's interesting, there always seems to be one of the three on guard at all times. They seem to have some sort of inborn sense not to be distracted by the actions of the other two. First it was Hams' job, and then while the two boys searched, it was Paps' responsibility and now it's Wills' turn. They are three parts functioning as one.*

Professor Adams at school would call it a survival mode—always protecting the unit, because if the unit collapses, then the individual parts perish also. Mike was fascinated by what he was experiencing.

Mike, suddenly became aware of the actions of Pap and Ham, he realized what Ham had found. *The boot print! They have found the boot print that I spotted earlier.*

"Take a look round," said Pap, "Air got ta be more sign. An don't fer git ta cheek both sides of the creek. Even round em logs thar."

The two boys followed Pap's instructions and began to search the area for more evidence of what direction the man who left the boot print had gone. Pap settled down on a flat rock jutting out of the ledge along the near side of the creek.

Mike took the opportunity to move, and slipped from tree to tree until he was near where the woods abruptly ended and the high rock ledge began. He checked the wind and determined that the light breeze of the afternoon had subsided to hardly any wind at all. What little air movement occurred was coming from his right, away from the three along the creek bed.

"Look like he's ma'be leafin the crick an headin fer the cabin; Pap" Will was looking in a northeastern direction, with a puzzled look on his face. "Ya don't guess he's know 'ear the cabin at do ya Pap?"

"No, he's don't, but if'in he's heedin thet 'rection, I's speck we'ens best catch em fer he's dis'overs the pelts thar."

"I's rec'on. Nothin else is thay boy?"

"No," replied Will as he motioned for Ham to join him at Pap's rock ledge seat.

"I's could use a bite ta eat," Ham said as he neared the ledge. "We'ens hafe eat nothin enny time ta day. We'ens left camp wit out eatin an I's gitin hongree."

"Ya a'ways hongree," piped in Will. "I's bet ya be hongree when thay take ya ta ya grave, ya weel."

Mike thought he saw a slight grin on the face of Ham's brother as he spoke. It was difficult to tell, as the three showed very little emotion either in their voice or facial expression. Mike continued to be intrigued by the three.

"Ta much gabbin, we'ens eat wit out a fire be fer an we'ens do it now Ham, dig out a couple dem packets an we'ens weel chow down on em cold an fast. En we'ens best be on 'ear way. We'ens need ta be gitin ta thet cabin."

Mike was astounded! *They are headed back to the cabin because they think that whoever made that boot print is headed that way. What do I do?*

If I follow them back to the cabin, I will be going the opposite direction that I think I should be going. And I will be going back to where I was before, back to their part of the country. I haven't any idea, who made that print, but they seem to know, and they also seem to be very concerned about him.

I would like to follow them and study their habits. I don't know why I didn't think of it before but they will make a great study for my research project next fall. I don't have a notebook or anything to write with, but maybe I can remember most of what they do. If I could be careful and not be seen, I could learn patterns on what they say and do. But leaving the stream is a risk, I would have to use the little compass; I don't want to get lost. Maybe if I mark my trail like Ruff described in one of his talks, I can find my way back to the stream. All it would take is my hunting knife on some trees and some stones to pile on each other.

I could do it. Why not? I can't be any worse off than I am. I don't know if I could find the campsite and I surely don't know where Ruff is now. For all I know, he may not even be in Roosevelt any more. He may have left. Mike waited for the three to head into the woods on the opposite shore and then proceeded to follow, being careful with every footstep he took.

CHAPTER 16

Having made excellent time, Ruff was in sight of the division office. Now hiking on a nearly level plain he had scaled most of the high ridge where the office was located. The sun was beginning to set in the western sky and in another half-hour or so he would have been hiking in the dark. There is always a greater hazard when hiking at night. Climbing up the high ridge would have been more treacherous because of the risk of stumbling and falling, or slipping and sliding down the steep incline. Ruff felt contentment with his achievement and the effort on the trail.

To establish a goal and then to meet that goal was something Ruff always admired in himself and in others. It was one of the things he hoped to instill in Mike during their camping excursion, but everything had mysteriously gone wrong and even Riff didn't know exactly what had happened. *What do I say to my sister? She will never believe how clumsily I have been. She will rocket right out of this world. And who is going to blame her. I can't believe it, so how is she going to believe it? And how do I explain all this to Bill? He could only hope that the friendship they enjoyed would be strong enough to withstand the inability to answer all of the questions that his friend would have for him.*

As it turned out, Bill wasn't at the office. Audrey, the office receptionist, had met Ruff on several different occasions, and was aware of the close bond between her boss and Ruff. She explained his absence.

"He had to appear in court today for the prosecution of a poaching case. He won't be back from Fort Collins until tomorrow afternoon. I know he will want to see you, Mr. Brindle. Would you like me to give him a call and let him know you're here?"

"Yes, would you please, it's kind of urgent."

"I'll see what I can do, I only hope he has his cell phone on, sometimes he goes into the courtroom and forgets to turn it back on when he comes out. Then I have to contact him by land phone first."

This is more information than I need right now, thought Ruff. Talkative, but efficient, Audrey soon had Ruff on the phone with his friend.

"Bill," Ruff began, "I ran into a little problem on the north trail." He then proceeded to explain the run-in with the three men at the campsite. He tried to answer Bill's questions as best he could.

"You say that you ran into them on the north trail? What where they doing, and where was this exactly?"

"It was about ten or fifteen miles southwest of the confluence of the Cache La Poudre and the Big Thompson Rivers, just south of the Poudre canyon." Ruff didn't know any other way to answer Bill's other question except to admit to the truth. "They were standing over me when I first saw them."

"What do you mean, standing over you? Were you hurt or something?"

"Well, I, er, must have passed out; I'm not sure what happened. Look Bill, can we not worry about that right now? It's a long story and I'd rather not go into it over the phone."

"Ruff, you're the one coming to me for help, I'm just trying to piece together what happened. I think it's important that I know what I am getting my rangers into if I send them out after these guys."

"You're right Bill, I'm sorry I can't give you a better answer. The truth is that I really don't remember what happened to me. I must have hit my head on something and—"

"And you haven't been to see a doctor yet, right? How long ago was this?"

"Well, that's another thing, I really don't know. It's been several days at least, I'm not sure."

"And you have been walking around the woods all this time with a possible concussion. Smart Ruff, real smart."

"Look, are we going to argue over my smarts, or are we going to try to catch these guys?" Ruff knew that his friend was egging him on a little and serious at the same time.

"Okay, okay, hand the phone back to Audrey so I can give her some instructions and you get some rest, you hear?"

"Huh, Bill, there is one other thing—I—huh—You know my sister's kid, my nephew, Mike? The one on my reservation. I—I have lost my nephew.

CHAPTER 17

By the time Ruff handed the phone to Audrey, he felt like a schoolboy who had just left the principal's office after a severe scolding. *I'm glad he is a friend, I wonder what he would be like as an enemy.* Ruff really didn't care to even speculate on that one.

Ruff had no question but that Bill would do everything in his power to help not only in tracking down the three men, but also in locating the whereabouts of Mike. Ruff knew that if anything happened to Mike he could never forgive himself, nor would his sister. Ruff glanced at Audrey as she scribbled notes down on her pad while talking to Bill. He was satisfied that Bill was already putting plans into action and assembling both men and equipment for the two searches that needed to take place simultaneously. Ruff knew that Bill's forces were well trained in the art of tracking the mischievous and the lost. Now there was nothing he could do except leave the operation in the hands of his buddy.

As soon as Audrey got off the phone, she turned to Ruff. "Bill says for you to go to his cabin, fix your self something to eat, and get some sleep. He's got a doctor coming up in the morning to take a look at you. Oh yes, he says to drink plenty of fluids. Now if you will excuse me, I have a ton of work to do before I can leave tonight. Here is the key to the cabin. You remember which one?"

Ruff nodded. "You just go on and get the wheels moving. Don't worry about me, I will take care of myself. And thanks for all your help." Ruff turned to leave.

"Oh, Mr. Brindle, don't you worry either, we'll find your nephew. Bill will be here by the time you wake in the morning, and he will see to that."

Ruff managed a smile and nodded again, as he let himself out the office door. Thinking to himself, Ruff wasn't so sure, *no one can really make that promise, but it's good to know they believe in their skills.* He let himself into the cabin and collapsed on the divan just inside the door. Not realizing the extent of his exhaustion, he was asleep before he even thought about taking off his boots.

Ruff awoke at a sound that came from the kitchen. It took a second for him to remember where he was and what had awakened him. It seemed like he had just laid down a few minutes earlier. A familiar voice came from the doorway of the cabin's kitchen.

"You don't follow orders very well, do you." It was a statement, not a question, and both he and Bill knew it. "You didn't have anything to eat last night, and from the looks of things you didn't drink any liquids either."

"Do you always wake your guests with such a ruckus? And since you mentioned it what's for breakfast?"

"We'll worry about your breakfast after Doctor Andrews takes a look at you. That's him just pulling in the drive now. Go let him in the door while I watch this bacon burn."

When Ruff opened the door, the doctor looked startled and took a couple of steps back. Then it dawned on Ruff that with several days' growth on his face, and his hair in disarray, and with him still wearing his old hiking clothes, he probably looked like something out of a horror movie.

"Don't be alarmed doc, the patient had a hard week." Said Bill from the kitchen doorway. "That's the guy I want you to take a look at. I suspect a concussion, but not sure how bad."

Re-gaining his composure, Doctor Andrews entered the cabin and motioned for Ruff to have a seat on the divan. After a short examination and asking Ruff several questions, such as, "Seeing double?" "Any headaches?" "How long ago did this happen?" "Experiencing any dizziness?" "Have you taken any medication?"

They were short questions so Ruff figured the doctor wanted short answers.

"No." "No." "I don't know." "No." "Some aspirin." The doctor raised an eyebrow at the "I don't know" answer, but let it pass. Ruff had earlier decided that unless specifically asked the sore ankle would go unmentioned.

Doctor Andrews turned to Bill. "I think he is okay, but if there is any change, get him to Fort Collins right away. Especially if any of his answers to my questions change." With that Doctor Andrews snapped his case shut, took another quizzical look at Ruff and turned to the cabin door.

"Thanks, Doc, send the bill to me, and never mind the appearance of the patient, the man needs a lot of work. Particularly in attitude and hygiene." Bill grinned at his own joke, while Ruff scowled and ignored his friend.

CHAPTER 18

Mike finished stacking the three rocks he had gathered from a nearby rock outcrop. Still following the three men who had been traveling for much of the morning, and with the bright sun overhead, Mike was thirsty. Deciding to sacrifice some of his precious water supply, he took a small gulp from his water bottle, being careful not to allow the sunlight to reflect off the bottle where it could be seen. After replacing the bottle in its belt holder his attention went back to the three men. They were discussing their own predicament—that of being short on water.

"Why ya not feel the can'ens lass nite fer ya went ta bed?" The old man asked. Neither of the boys seemed eager to answer it. Finally Will spoke up.

"I's figger we'ens would hafe time this mornin ta take care of thet. But we'ens left the camp in a hurry, Pap. Thar no time fer enny water boilin."

"An now thar ain't no water, is thar?" Mike noticed the old man didn't turn loose of a point easily. "Weel, we'ens got ta git ta our cabin, so's best be gitin. Drenk ken wait."

Mike had marked his trail and was ready to continue stalking the three subjects, as he referred to them in the mental notes he was making for himself. When they moved, he moved, always mindful of doing so in complete silence and without being sighted by any of the three pair of eyes that were constantly on the alert for anything suspicious around them. As he slipped from tree to tree he glanced back at the three rocks. *As soon as I begin to lose sight of them I need to mark a tree.* When a decision was made that a tree needed to be marked, Mike would do so down near the ground where it would be less conspicuous. Remembering Ruff's advice in one of his talks that Mike had heard several times, *you won't be the only one in the woods, and others may notice the marked trees. That's a dead give-away that you are there, so if you don't want to be followed, be careful how you mark your tree.* Noticing that his subjects were moving at a faster pace now, Mike realized the need to speed up a bit. But at the same time he reminded himself that speed meant more of a chance of making unnecessary noise—noise that would alert the subjects of his presence.

Suddenly, the three veered off in a different direction. *I have to stop and make a stack of three stones to show the change. I will have to be quick about it or they will get too far ahead of me and I can't risk rushing to catch up with them.* Mike hurriedly stacked his stones, placing an extra one on the ground in the direction of the change. There, now, if I can read my own markings, I will be able to re-trace my route if I need to. The three men changed direction three more times in the mile or so they had covered. *What are they doing?* Mike was puzzled. *It's almost as if they are making a wide u-turn and heading back. Back! That's what they're doing, they're back-tracking like they did when I was with them. If they back—track the same trail, they might see my marks. What will they do then? Come searching for me probably.* Mike knew he was in trouble if the men detected his presence and they decided to stalk the stalker.

Racking his brain for some way out of his predicament, Mike thought about what Ruff would do. *Ruff would take the easy way out. He would simply slip off the trail, find a good hiding place and wait for his pursuers to complete their back-tracking maneuver and let them come back to him. Yeah! I can do that too,—if I can slip away and find a good hiding place.* Mike headed to his right toward one of the many rock outcrops encountered in the park, and finding an indention in a rock face that was partially hidden by a large boulder, he dragged some downed tree limbs to one side and slipped into his "cave." *There, now all I have to do is wait. Yeah, wait and see if this works and if it doesn't? What then? Ruff, you didn't cover that in your lecture, did you?*

CHAPTER 19

For what seemed like an eternity, Mike watched from his hiding place. It had probably only been about an hour in real time when the stalker realized his subjects were returning. Spotting the three men coming through the woods, Mike was somewhat surprised that his ruse had apparently worked. *Now what?* To far away to hear, Mike became anxious when the three stopped and began a discussion. *They've found something; I wonder what it could be? Wait, it is the rocks, the ones I just made to show the change in direction we took on the trail. They've found out that someone is following them. I wish I could hear what they are saying.* Mike felt he had no choice except to sit tight and wait to see what the three men would do about their discovery.

He didn't have long to wait as the three soon separated and each moved in a different direction away from the location of the pile of rocks. Will moved to the left of the rocks about one hundred yards, then disappeared from view. Pap went about the same distance back down the trail in the direction from which they had all came. And Ham came straight toward where Mike sat hidden. Halting about the same distance from the rocks as the other two, Ham slipped behind a tree putting it between him and the location of the rocks. When Mike saw Ham squat down, he realized that that must have been what Will had done when he disappeared from Mike's view.

Ham was less than fifty feet from Mike and in full view, though hidden from anyone coming up the trail. The three waited. So did Mike. After about an hour, Mike noticed Pap coming back up the trail and motioned for the two sons to come towards him. When the three had collected together again they had a short discussion, which Mike was not able to hear, and then started off in the original direction they had taken when Mike set up the rock marker earlier. By now the sun was well into the afternoon sky, and the three were moving at a fast pace.

I'll bet that they are anxious to get to the cabin, and I think I know why. They still have two cub bear hides there. That would be strong evidence of poaching, which could get them a hefty fine and maybe some time in jail. That's probably more important to them right now than finding out who is on their trail. For some reason, they don't seem to be too concerned about the fact that somebody was marking their trail. I wonder why is that? Maybe they have already decided they know who is following them. They may think that it is someone of no consequence that the three of them can handle. Maybe someone they have already dealt with in some way . . .

It was still daylight when the trio, with Mike following, arrived at the cabin. Mike darted behind a tree just as the men halted, dropped their knapsacks and turned to take a hard look back toward the way they had come. By the time Mike was brave enough to peer out from around his tree, the three were at the water well and Ham was hauling up a bucket of water by way of a rope tied to it. Mike immediately realized how thirsty he was, but knew his thirst was something he could not quench at that moment.

As Mike watched, Emma opened the cabin door and looked out at the three. She didn't say a word. Leaving the cabin door open she went to the pile of wood that was at the corner of the shack and loaded her arms with kindling and carried it back into the cabin. The door still open, she re-emerged with a pail and walked to where the three were still slating their thirst. She took the bucket from Ham and dropped it back into the well. She then proceeded to pull up the full bucket, hand over hand, with an apparent ease that amazed Mike. Pouring the water from the bucket to the pail, she dropped the bucket on the ground and picking up the full pail, walked back to the cabin closing the door behind her. Mike noticed that this entire operation occurred without Emma looking at, or saying anything to, any of the three men.

Without comment or emotion of any kind, Ham picked up the bucket and dropped it into the well for the third time. When he pulled it out, the three took turns, with Pap first, dipping their heads in the bucket and shaking off the excess water with a rapid back and forth head movement. By the time they were through at the well, Mike noticed a stream of smoke coming from the chimney of the cabin. The three trudged toward its door, all three with their empty hands stuffed deep in their pockets.

Emma is fixing something for them to eat; however these three came home without any game. I bet they don't say anything about the food she places before them this evening. Mike smiled as he pictured the three looking at a bland non-descript plate of food. *Probably potatoes, turnips, and greens,* his grin widened, as he added, *no meat!.*

By the time things settled down at the cabin, it was nearly dark. Mike decided to chance a trip to the water well and fill his water bottle. With the three inside, he figured that they were more than likely to stay inside for a while. It had been a long day and Mike needed something to eat and drink. After filling up with water he decided to pull back into the woods and finding a spot out of sight of the cabin and protected from the trail leading to it. He relished the comfort of a fire, but without matches and no sunshine, he had no way of starting a fire. Besides, a fire in the woods at night would surely attract some attention if anyone were about.

Selecting a couple pieces from his food supply, he chewed slowly and completely. Aware that it wasn't enough to satisfy his degree of hunger, but knowing it would have to do for now, Mike settled in for the night. Finding a large boulder still warm from the daylight sun and leaned his back to it. The warmth was soothing to him and soon fell asleep. He slept soundly. So soundly that he didn't hear the rustling of some nearby bushes. A large shadow appeared amid the trees, but Mike's sleep was too deep to be disturbed by shadows.

CHAPTER 20

Peering over the shoulder of his good friend, Ruff pointed to a spot on the map spread out before the four of them. With the two was Captain Edward Russell, of the Colorado Ranger Division who, just the month before, had been transferred in from a unit in Utah. Also in the group was Lieutenant Robert Summers, a superior tracker.

"Our campsite was right here near the rocky ridge on the East Side of the tributary," Ruff explained. "That's where I ran into the three men for the second time. I don't know what set them off but they were in a foul mood when they entered the camp. They practically held me at gunpoint demanding something to eat and drink. I offered them tea. Green tea."

Bill shook his head, "You never were one to leave a situation well enough alone. You say they had a shotgun, did you notice the make or gauge?"

"It looked like an old Remington, very plain, no frills, but a double barrel and it looked like a 12 gauge. I never could determine if it was loaded or not. From the way the old man acted, I would advise that we assume it to be loaded."

Bill drew a circle the size of a quarter around the spot Mike had indicated. "Now where did you come across them the first time?"

"That's a little tricky, I'm not sure. I think it had to be somewhere northwest of the tributary, about here." Again Ruff pointed to a spot on the map, and Bill drew another circle. "I know it was near Indian Lookout Point. That's where I injured myself somehow. I am not sure what happened, but things are a little fuzzy for most of that day."

"Things are usually a little fuzzy where you're concerned, aren't they? I bet you tripped over your own two feet and bumped your head on a rock and you don't want to admit it. Am I right?" Ruff looked at his friend, trying to determine if he was chiding him or if he could be serious.

"At least I know enough not to stand up in a canoe while it is floating in five feet of river water. Like some people I know."

"Couldn't you two hold this discussion on your relative wilderness skills at some other time? Right now we need to concentrate on the problems at hand," Captain Russell interjected. "Particularly about where these three renegades are. Where do you suggest we start looking for your nephew?"

Ruff nodded his head. "You're right, sorry about the distraction. All I can tell you is that Mike left the creek campsite. I have no idea why or where he might have gone."

"Let's get started on that situation first. Lieutenant, why don't you take Sergeant Douglas's squad and head down to the campsite and see what you can find? If you come across any indication of where the boy went, then pursue it from there. In the meantime, I will go with these two comedians, and we'll try to get a trace on those other three. Does that meet with your approval, Bill?"

"Everything except putting me in the same category as this crazy varmint."

All four of the men chuckled at the gnarly face Ruff made in response to Bill's remark.

*   *   *

The ride had been an uncomfortable one, and after an unusually rough bump, Ruff could not resist. "You missed one back there, Captain."

"That's all right, I'll get it on the way back." Driving the ranger vehicle Captain Russell kept a sharp eye on the road and wasn't about to take much gruff from any of the four men in the vehicle. Sitting in the front passenger seat, Bill Waddle had a map across his lap. Trying to read it and examine the surrounding area while in the vehicle was difficult. Behind him in the back seat was Ruff, who had kept a running dialogue of Captain Russell's driving ability. Bill had never experienced a time when Ruff didn't have a comment to make and this was no exception. Beside Ruff sat Charles "Charlie" Jones, a new comer to the district ranger unit, with a reputation as an excellent tracker.

About that time Ruff let out a cry, "Stop this thing and back up!"

"Now what? You want me to hit another pothole?" The captain slowed but did not stop.

"Just do as I say, I think I spotted something back there."

"Ruff, if this is another one of your jokes—" Bill chimed in.

"No joke, Bill, I want to check something out back there between those three trees."

With a nod from Bill, Captain Russell stopped and backed the vehicle to the point Ruff had indicated to him. All four of the men piled out of the carryall and followed Ruff to a spot among the trees.

"There it is, I thought I saw it as we flew past." Ruff paid no attention to the power of the Canyon River District that he had gathered about him: District Superintendent Bill Waddle, Ranger Captain Edward Russell, and Charles Jones, a ranger first class. The four men surrounded the three rocks piled neatly one on top of each other with a fourth rock on the north side of the pile.

"What do you make of it, Charlie?" Ruff knew that Jones was supposed to be second only to Lieutenant Summers, in tracking abilities.

"Well, it's a poor location for a marker. Too much out in the open to be placed here by someone who knows what they are doing. The rocks don't look natural in their setting; they look like they have been deliberately placed here. Any one who knows how to trail would know what they represent. I think we have a trail being set by an amateur. Maybe a Boy Scout leaving a trail for a buddy."

"I wonder—" Ruff didn't finish his thought.

"Ruff, why don't you and Charlie follow this trail and see if you can find out any more about what is going on here. Captain Russell and I will proceed on up to thunder point, that high ridge there, and see if we can come up with anything. If either of us finds evidence of the boy, give a shout on the phones." Without waiting for a reply, Bill got into the ranger carryall and motioned for Captain Russell to take the front passenger seat.

"See you in a bit." Ruff saluted his friend, and started studying the ground as ranger Jones did the same. Bill and the Captain roared off toward the northwest.

After about forty-five minutes searching, Charlie called to Ruff. He was knelling beside a tree. "I think I found something here. There's a mark on this tree that looks freshly made. It's down near the bottom like someone was trying to keep it from being seen."

"That's in line with the rock pile. I can barely make out the rocks down by those trees. Somebody was definitely trying to lay out a trail here. How old do you think these marks are, Charlie?"

"Not more than a day or so. They look pretty fresh. Maybe less than a day. Let's continue on and see if we can get a line on who it is and how many there are. I'm going to call in to the office and get a list of reservations we have in this part of the forest. Maybe we will be lucky and come up with a short list." The ranger pulled his radio out of his pocket and proceeded to punch in numbers. Ruff, in the meantime decided to explore the area for any evidence that might tell them more.

CHAPTER 21

Sniffing the air, the old sow continued her search for food. Being a camp bear, she wasn't exactly hungry, but had an inner urgency to continue feeding on whatever she could find. She had an innate desire she couldn't explain. Even if she could she had to satisfy her craving for food. Having inherited very keen eyesight, and as opposed to many animals, her ability see the different colors that abounded around her she also possessed a very good sense of hearing. But it was her sense of smell that was exceptional, often surprising herself with what she could "read" in one sniff of air. Like now, when she detected nothing in the air that would appear as a threat to her, neither did she "taste" anything in the air that indicated food was near except the many green plants and the dried berries on the abundant bushes in the area.

Food, of course, was the real reason for sniffing the air. Food was what interested her the most. However, she was also glad to know that the area was clear of any threat. That meant that she was free to go back to her search for food, after all, that was her number one priority. Especially now that her cubs were no longer with her. Automatically swinging her head from side to side she expected them to be there. They were not, and she couldn't explain to herself what had happened. She had heard the gunshots, but not knowing what they represented, except for being extremely loud, she didn't make a connection between her cub's disappearance and the sound. She later found their scent but that didn't lead her to them. Just to a bare spot in the woods that was mixed with human scent.

Now she was on full alert as she was outside her usual feeding territory. She wasn't too worried however, as she knew that the bear whose territory she had invaded would gladly share her food if there were plenty to eat. But the she-bear that claimed the territory didn't always agree that there was sufficient food for both bears and they would fight over it. But it seemed like there was always plenty to eat, given the wide range of foods that appealed to her. It was just that it seemed like there was never enough of the rich food and never enough time to search for better things to eat. No matter how much she ate, it didn't seem to satisfy her craving for food, she wanted more. As a black bear, she was very smart and also very adept at solving problems, which again, usually centered on food. By accidental encounters, she had found that the human scent, was nothing to be trusted, and she would usually give them wide range. Occasionally, a human would get too close to her or the cubs, and she would get upset with them, but the human scent usually meant food. The best two kinds of food: the sweet kind, and the easy kind. She had to admit that when it came to food she had a sweet tooth. Her favorite was honey, and the food that went with it, such as bee larva. The sweeter the better. It was even worth getting stung by the bees, just for a helping of that honeycomb. There weren't too many places on her where a bee could get a good sting. Her nose, eyelids, and the tips of her ears were all. She often got even with the bees by eating several while getting at the honey. She had learned to use her lips, teeth, and claws efficiently as tools to gain food such as honey. Another nice thing about honey, it was easy food. She didn't like having to work too hard for her meals.

That was something else she liked about humans, their food was usually easy food. She usually had success in opening picnic baskets, ice coolers, and even backpacks. Most garbage cans were no problem for her. She once even managed to get into an unlocked and unattended automobile.

Being a black bear meant that she was "omnivorous," which didn't mean anything to her, but she knew that she would eat all kinds of plants and animals. She liked rodents, leaves, roots, berries, nuts, and even grass. Her agility at climbing trees to get acorns and hickory nuts was unequalled by any animal her size. Also digging for sweet roots with her mighty claws, and pick berries from the bush with those same claws was an easy task.

She had two favorite oak trees in her own territory, that she returned to every year, climbing high into the trees to feast on their acorns. She didn't know how she remembered, but she knew where they were in her territory and the nuts on her trees were the sweetest ever.

She would consume any animal she could catch. From tiny ants, grubs, and insects, to such things as frogs and fish, and even young deer, and elk. There was no objection on her part to even feed on dead animals of any size and during any time of the year. The only exception to this was during hibernation. There would be no feeding during that time of the year.

Suddenly the old sow froze. She knew that she had heard something. What was it? Listening intently, she moved through the brush toward where she thought the sound had came. Stopping to listen again, she heard nothing at first, then there it was again. Being a black bear, she couldn't recognize a human cough. She heard human voices. That was something she recognized and her instinct cautioned her to be a little fearful of humans. They were untrustworthy, first offering food, then trying to withhold it, to her it was a frustrating situation, they couldn't have it both ways. Then they would often hit you on the nose with something that would hurt.

Now the sow had decided to slip back into the woods. Suddenly, the breeze that had been coming from her backside switched direction, and she caught a faint, but familiar scent of her cub, mixed with the scent of humans.

Her great sense of smell told her that one of her cubs was nearby. Through no fault of her own she was not aware of the fact that she unknowingly picked up the scent still being carried by a harmless person. Someone who was forced to drape her cub's pelt over his shoulders and carry it back to a cabin. Thinking of nothing else but the protection of her cubs, the mother charged through the bushes toward the familiar scent. She charged blindly and with a vengeance.

CHAPTER 22

"Over here," Ruff called to Charlie, "I think I have something."

Charlie hurried to the large rock outcrop where Ruff was standing. "Take a look at this. What do you see?"

Charlie studied the area, then in response to Ruff's question, replied. "I think someone spent some time in this indentation, and not too long ago, either. Look at this; see where they dragged the tree limbs over to this side to protect themselves from being seen by either someone or something. It obstructs the vision of anyone coming back up the trail so they could have been hiding from someone. Look at the size of the space in the indention, it's not big enough for you, so it has to be just one person and that person must have been smaller than you or I are, Ruff."

"By golly, you are good, son. You said that this occurred recently. How did you arrive at that?" Ruff said, impressed with Charlie's tracking skills.

"Well, for one thing, look at the scrapes in the loose dirt, the wind hasn't had time to fill the furrows completely back in with silt. Also the tips of the tree branches, where they were dragged across the rock and dirt, are still clean. The sun hasn't had time to dry them out, and they're not crusted over. I would bet that this hidey-hole was used yesterday, probably yesterday afternoon."

"Geez, if you are somehow proved to be correct, that's pretty good work for a city kid." Ruff had read Charlie's resume on Bill's desk that morning. He knew that Charlie grew up in the south side of Chicago.

"I didn't spend my whole life pounding cement sidewalks," Charlie replied with a big boyish grin on his face.

"Well now, let's see what we have so far. We've got two parties, don't know if they know each other or not. One party is following the other, and the second party is trying to mark the trail of the first party or trying to mark his own trail. Maybe the second party is afraid of the first party for some reason, or maybe the first party did something to the second party." Ruff looked at Charlie to see if he was following his reasoning.

"Or maybe the first party is much larger or stronger in some way, than the second party." Added Charlie.

"Good point," said Ruff. "We also know that both parties are only a day or less ahead of us.

"That's if I'm right," Charlie mused, "maybe we should say we 'think' they're just a day or less ahead of us."

"I'll give you that, Charlie, but in my sixty plus years, I've learned to trust my instincts. And my instincts tell me that you have good instincts."

"I think I followed that line of reasoning." Charlie grinned again. "We also know that the second party was not too swift in the trail-marking department. But he was a quick thinker in the 'making a hidey-hole' department, I'd say."

"I'll give you that one too," Ruff said with admiration.

After exploring the area for another fifteen minutes they decided to move slowly up the trail and continued to look for signs that would provide answers to their questions. Ruff found a partial boot print of a small size. He believed that reinforced the theory that at least one of the people on the trail was rather small. About one hundred yards or so further up the trail from the last marked tree, Charlie found another. Indeed, someone was clearly trying to mark his trail for whatever reason.

Charles Jones and Ruff Brindle were fast becoming a good team of trackers. They were also becoming fast friends. It was a hard call to predict which of them would find the latest clue revealing the activities of the two unknown parties that were moving somewhere ahead of them on the trail.

"I think I know where this trail is going to lead," Charlie proclaimed. But Ruff was not to be outdone. "Me too. There is a box canyon just over that far ridge there to the northwest. I think that is where we are headed."

"It's the only large box canyon in the area and the best place to hide out."

"What leads you to believe that one of these two parties wants to hide out?" Ruff asked, his curiosity piqued. "What did you notice that would indicate that?"

There was neither pride nor aristocracy in Charlie's voice as he responded, "I think that the first party knows that someone is trailing them. About an hour back we found evidence that they back-trailed their own trail. They couldn't help but notice the misplaced rock markers and if they are trail smart enough to back-track themselves, then they know they are being stalked by whoever party number two is.

"Now if you know someone's on your trail and you don't set a trap for them, why? Because you have more important things to take care of, or you know that there is a place where you can deal with your pursuers on your own terms. I figure that party number one is in a big hurry to get to a safe place. Safe because they know that they have the upper hand."

"And that means—?" Ruff figured his tracking partner was way ahead of him and ready for the question.

"It means that party number one has a hide out already set up and traps laid for the second party to fall into. And that leads us to the box canyon."

"Charlie, you are something else. I have no doubt that what you surmise is pretty accurate. What intuition you have! Where did you get your instincts?"

"Probably from my paternal grandmother. She was half Osage Indian, but before we start patting ourselves on the back, we better have the facts. Let's get to that canyon first, and prove our theory. Then maybe we will find out whom we are dealing with and why all this cloak and dagger stuff is going on anyway."

"I think," Ruff interjected, "you better get on that radio and contact Bill and that lieutenant of his. We may need all the back up we can muster, when we get to the box end of that canyon. Remember that there are people out here carrying double-barreled 12-gauge shotguns. We don't have any thing to match that kind of firepower."

"I agree," replied Charlie, "Captain Russell better be notified and informed of our read on this thing. Better to go in prepared and not need it, than to need it and not be prepared."

Spoken like a true wilderness man, Ruff thought nodding his head in agreement, and replied with: "Amen."

CHAPTER 23

Ham stood over Mike with an old, but freshly sharpened corn knife. In other parts of the world, it would have been called a machete. By any name it meant the same to Mike. One swing to the neck would be all that was needed. Will stood a few feet away with Pap's double barreled shotgun in the crook of his arms.

From the amount of light in the sky, Mike guessed it was near daybreak. There was enough light to see the two sons, and he could just barely make out the faces. Mike had slept little during the night, what with his nearness to the cabin, and the strange, always changing shadows of the night, he dared not close his eyes. The noise from his growling stomach, due to the lack of a good meal in recent days aided his inability to sleep. However, he finally dozed off shortly before daybreak, and Ham had nudged him awake with the corn knife to his ribs.

"Ya thot ya were smart, boy." Ham listened silently to his brother, while maintaining his control of Mike. "We'ens sat a trap, an ya feel rite en it. Ya tink we'ens did'dent know ya rite behind when we'ens git ta cabin. boy? Ya tink we'ens thet dumm, boy? Even Emma spied ya when she got wood. Pap said, 'jest wait a whiilst an he weel be hiden in the woods. An rite enough, 'ear ya are."

It took Mike a while to figure out what was happening, as he thought his movements had gone undetected by the family in the cabin. He now realized how wrong he was and that he faced serious trouble and no one to come to his aid.

Mike had been staring at Will, trying to follow his words. At the same time he was keeping a close watch on Ham. As Will finished his story, Mike glanced at Ham, and for the first time since his encounter with the three, thought he saw a slight smile cross Ham's face.

After a short pause, Will spoke up again, "Pap's upset wit ya boy, ya caused we'ens enough trouble, not ta talk bout the food ya et. We'ens don't feed enny lit'le boy thet come by. We'ens barly hafe enough fer 'ear own. Pap said ya got ta diss'pear, en now is good a time as enny."

At that, Mike noticed a slight movement from Ham as he glanced at his brother. Ham objected to Will's suggestion as to the fate of their prisoner. "Pap ne'er said ta keel em. He's jest wont em ta diss'pear. He did'dent—"

This was the first time Mike had heard Ham challenge Will's authority. And Will didn't allow it.

"Butt up, Ham, an ya jest feelow 'rections. I's do the tinkin when Pap not round. Ya **read** me boy?"

Ham's eyes immediately dropped to the ground, and with his head down to his chest, he nodded with great movement of his head. Will stared intently at the youngster. In the dimness of the early morning light, he strained to see that Ham acknowledged his instructions. It was a practiced move and Mike could only guess that Ham had responded to his older brother in the same manner, many times over.

"Now I's tink it time we'ens take this boy ta top of the box en of this canon. One miss step en ya tumble all the way down the back side." Will looked at his brother. "Thet be fen, boy?"

Ham again nodded his head. "Thet be a fall wot would broke some bone. Not one whar enny one weel walk out."

"I's done talk boy, now git movin. Will swung the shotgun to indicate the direction he wanted Mike to walk.

But, before Mike could make a move, a huge she-bear came rushing out of the brush behind Will. A black sow bear at full charge was a terrible sight. Particularly if she is headed straight for you, and this bear was making a beeline toward Mike. Will was between Mike and the bear. With one swipe of her massive right paw, she knocked Will out of the way with such force that she surly broke his neck. Will tumbled into the brush and his prone body lay still. The shotgun Will had been carrying flew through the air to end up at the feet of both Ham and Mike. Both boys were frozen to his spot about ten yards from where Will had stood just a moment before. The old sow stopped in her tracks, apparently surprised at the disappearance of the human she had swatted. Standing on her hind legs, she rose to her full height for a better view of the two humans still in front of her. She let out a roar, dropped to all fours and started swinging her head back and forth.

It seemed to Mike, she was looking for something, something that wasn't there. It was then that Mike noticed the limp. The bear had an injured front left paw. The cub's mother, Mike muttered to himself. Suddenly Ham, whose feet seemed to have taken root, and whose eyes had been transfixed on the prone still form of his brother, came to life. With the corn knife raised high over his head, he rushed the bear.

Mike mouthed the word "no" but not a sound came out. As Ham approached, the old sow once again raised to a massive height from on her hind legs. The knife, wielded by someone who seemed used to swinging it, was true to its mark. It caught the bear across the nose and face; it cut deep into the flesh. At the same time, she closed her great jaws around the soft tissue of Ham's throat. The old sow ripped a mouth full of living tissue from his throat.

Ham looked squarely into the eyes of the bear for a split second and then collapsed into the grasp of the front paws. Taking another hold with her massive jaws, the great animal clamped down on Ham's throat once again and whipped her head back and forth. Ham's head flopped around like on a rag doll, as it nearly separated from the rest of the body. Only the skin and exposed neck bones held it to the body.

At that point, Mike could only guess what took place in the mind of the bear. Suddenly the intense pain from the machete chop across her nose and face seemed to take effect. She released her hold on Ham. Glancing around, as if searching one more time, the bear whirled to inspect Mike. By this time, Mike had picked up the shotgun and pointed it at the bear. But the animal seemed to have had enough human contact for the time and spun back around to leave quickly in the direction it had come. The attack had taken less than five minutes but left a trail of death and mayhem in its wake.

Mike stood, speechless. It seemed an eternity, before he could move, but in reality was only a couple of minutes. It was only then that he noticed the old man standing at the edge of the trees. His face with out expression. Instinctively, Mike hefted the shotgun to his waist, then pointed the barrel away from "Pap" when he realized that the old man was apparently unarmed.

He was not a "gun" person, but about a year ago, when Mike had turned eighteen, Ruff had insisted that he know how to use different types of weapons. At first, Jennie was adamant in her refusal to allow Ruff to teach Mike how to fire a gun. But after much pleading and a few good points on why Mike needed to learn from Ruff, and not from someone who didn't respect the weapons they used, she relented.

Ruff introduced Mike to his first weapon, the pistol Mike's grandfather had carried in WWII—the well-known .38 Smith and Wesson Victory Model. They practiced at the public firing range and Mike's skill with the weapon was so erratic that it left Ruff shaking his head.

Then they tried the rifle. At the time, Ruff was using a bolt action, Springfield .30-06 rifle for deer hunting. It had a rosewood stock and a blued finish. Though Mike liked the feel and look of the rifle, his marksmanship was mediocre. Ruff's comment was "you need lots of practice."

The last weapon that Ruff had for Mike was the shotgun. It was a Mossberg 20-gauge 500 Bantam model that Ruff had in his collection. It was a "youth" model, but Ruff thought it was the one for Mike to learn on. It had a specially shortened stock designed for smaller framed shooters. In addition, the forefend was positioned closer to the shooter for easier operation. Just the thing for the youngster, Ruff thought. Mike fell in love with the gun. Ruff had equipped it with a plug so that it would fire only a single shot. Mike fired the gun so much that to save time Ruff explained the precautions to Mike and removed the plug.

Mike did not become very proficient with any of the three weapons, but enjoyed shooting clays with the 20-gauge shotgun. It was fun.

Now, he knew, wasn't a time for fun. As far as he could tell, the old man was unarmed, but Mike was still extremely cautious as he watched to see what the old man would do. Though about fifteen yards away from Mike, the old man spoke in a matter-of-fact monotone voice.

"I's want ta cheek on the boys." He approached the spot where Will lay, and knelt down. Will had not moved and from the look on the old man's face, Mike knew Will wasn't going to be moving on his own any more. If medical aid had been available, they would have told the father that his son died of asphyxiation. When the bear struck the boy, she shattered the fourth and fifth cervical vertebra that in turn sliced into the spinal cord. This rendered Will incapable of breathing. He was beyond help minutes after the blow from the bear.

The old man patted his son's head a couple of times and remained kneeling for several minutes. Then he stood, and slowly made his way over to where Ham lay. Even from his viewing point, Mike knew that Ham was dead as his head was practically ripped from his body. The bear, in its rage had ripped the carotid and occipital arteries of the neck. She had torn apart the jugular vein, and numerous smaller vessels. In addition to that damage, the savage and powerful jaws had destroyed all seven vertebrae that make up the spine in the human neck.

Maybe the bear had not intended death, but its instincts were a very compelling force. The old man once again knelt beside the body of a son and peered into empty eyes. When he finally straightened and stood, Mike tensed and gripped the shotgun a little tighter. The old man took a long look at Mike. After a time, in which Mike assumed he was deciding what to do with him, the old man finally spoke.

"I's do ya no harm, son, I's got ta bury the boys. I's got nothing left ta fite fer. I's go back ta the cabin fer the shevel. Ya ken feelow ef'in ya wont."

With that he went into the woods and Mike had no choice except to follow. He had the gun, but they both knew he was not in control.

As they neared the cabin, the old man let out a whoop. Emma came to the door and peered at the two. Mike could sense her concern that he was carrying the gun. But it apparently meant little to her as she looked back at the old man.

"The boys 'ear deed," he said to her, "the bar got em both. I's be bury em 'ear thay's lay. Ya mit git the pick an come help, ef'in ya care ta."

Then the old man picked up a spade leaning against the cabin wall and proceeded to retrace his steps. Emma glanced along the side of the cabin wall, where a well-used pickax was leaning on the cabin. She looked back at Pap, and back at the pickax, as if she was telling him, *Hey, no way am I picking that up. You get it if you want it.* Pap said nothing and neither did Emma. Pap turned again to take care of his sons.

"Just a minute, there," Mike blurted out without any forethought. "I think we ought to wait and contact the rangers. Don't we need to tell them what happened so that they can determine that there was no foul play involved in the deaths of your two sons?"

"Ya ken contack enny ya want. I's got ta bury the boys. At least, Mike's question had kept the old man from leaving.

"But that's just my point," Mike pleaded. "The bear killed them; the rangers will have to verify that in their report to the authorities."

"Wot this words mean? Ver'fy an ath—ath'orys?"

Mike searched his mind for words to explain to the old man that he couldn't just bury the bodies and be done with it.

"I mean—" Mikes' attempt to explain was cut off by Emma, who was still standing by the open door.

"Et sees like the boy hafe a pont," she interjected.

"Wot he's pont?" Mike was relieved. *At least we are getting him to listen. But I don't know for how long. We have to keep him from burying Ham and Will.*

Emma said. "He's pont thet we'ens need ta contack the Mashell so's he's ken sees Ham and Will be keel by the bar an not by ya, hem, or I's."

Mike was impressed by Emma's way of explaining a complex problem in such simple words. "She's right," he said.

"Ya don't use the boys names a'oud enny more. Thay deed."

It took Mike a moment to digest what Pap was talking about. When it dawned on him what Pap meant, he was amazed. *It's true.* Mike recalled a discussion that took place in a folklore class in school. The instructor explained that in some cultures it was taboo to say the deceased's name aloud, ever again. Members of the culture could refer to the deceased as "one" or "my" or another pronoun, but never their given name. He explained it had something to do about invoking evil spirits, and preventing the soul from entering the spirit world. *I never expected to meet someone who really believed in that stuff. This will make great research material for my project. I must remember what the old man said.*

Mike's thoughts were interrupted when Pap replaced the shovel against the cabin wall. It was only then that Mike realized the old man had been standing still with a puzzled look on his face. Apparently, the man had been mulling over what Emma had told him about the Marshall, and had come to the conclusion that she was right.

I guess the old fellow is going to listen to reason, Mike mused to himself. *Now, if we can come up with some way of getting the bodies back to the cabin, figure out some way to contact the authorities, er Marshall, we would be home free. Easy to say.*

"How do we get the boys back to the cabin?" Mike was proud of himself; hopefully he had set the old man's thinking back to a positive one and kept from invoking the evil spirits at the same time.

"We'ens got ta make a travois ta tote em. "We'ens could of use the one wot take back the bar meat. But Emma done chop it fer kin'lin. Ya know how ta make a travois, boy?"

Mike shook his head. "No but I can learn." *Think positive Mike.*

With that the old man set out to explain, and show Mike, the art of travois making. All it took was some long semi-straight tree limbs and wild vines, to use for rope, from the woods. After finishing the travois, the old man retrieved the harness that he had fashioned on the trail to haul the bear meat back to the cabin.

"Air, we'ens ken git ta work, boy. Ya wont somptin ta eat frist, boy?

Mike nodded, he was famished. *Even bear stew would taste good right now.*

As the two entered the cabin, Mike took every opportunity to look around, without being too obvious about it, and place in his memory the contents of the cabin. That didn't amount to much, Mike reflected, as he glanced around the sparsely outfitted one room structure.

CHAPTER 24

It was well after mid-morning. The day following the call Charlie made to Bill, found both Bill and Captain Russell officially standing in front of two squads of Colorado Forest Rangers and four agents from the Colorado Bureau of Investigation, all assembled at a point leading into a large box canyon. In addition, the group was re-enforced by two troopers from the Colorado Highway Patrol, and the Larimer County Sheriff, Benny Crocker. Sheriff Crocker had a drug sniffing Collie dog named Boots at the end of a leash that was always too short and pulled straight as an arrow. Off to one side Charlie Jones and Ruff, surveyed the collected force.

Ruff looked at the assemblage, dropped his head, shook it, and glanced at Charlie. "Words over the radio must travel fast. How did all these agencies get involved? Charlie, I hope we're right about this, because I never saw such fire power in one spot before since they lit the candles on my birthday cake last year." Charlie's grin matched Ruffs'.

"I hear you, but as I remember, this was your idea, not mine."

"With this group it might take more than two hours to reach the box end of the canyon. You and I could accomplish the same thing in one hour."

Situated in front of the group, Bill turned to Captain Russell, and said, "We better get this bunch headed in the right direction. Tell them to pass the word that they are to make as little noise as possible. Every man make sure to keep the person on their left and right in sight. And remind them that they are not to shoot until I say so, or unless they are fired upon. Make sure that is clear to everyone, and I mean everyone." He pointed directly at Ruff when he reached the end of his instructions.

"Okay, let's move out." Bill swung his right arm forward in an over-handed motion. The move up the canyon was on. No one in the group had any idea what they were headed into.

*   *   *

The "invasion force" as Ruff had named it, was over halfway into the canyon when Bill called a halt.

"He turned to Captain Russell, and announced his instructions so every body could hear. "Thirty minutes. We'll take a thirty-minute break. Don't go hog-wild with the canteens. You may need water worse later than now, so go easy. No smoking. The canyon is dry, and I don't want to risk a forest fire."

Bill moved over to the tree where Ruff and Charlie were sitting with their backs against it. "Ruff, I want to let you know that I heard from Lieutenant Summers, and they have had no luck in locating Mike. Sergeant Douglas's squad has done a good job staying with the assignment. They think that he left the camp and struck out for the back country by mistake. So they are going to move their search to that part of the park. It is a large area and will take time to do a proper search. I want you to know that if Mike is there, Robert Summers is the man to find him. Are you fine with that, Ruff?"

Not wanting to offer information that might be misleading, Ruff kept his private thoughts on the subject to himself. "I know that Lieutenant Summers is a good man. I have confidence in his abilities as a tracker. And Sergeant Douglas is the best when it comes to leading a squad, Let's hope they're successful."

Bill took a hard look at Ruff thinking; *that was too easy, Ruff is holding something back for whatever reason. But if that is true, then he must have good cause and I guess I'll have to respect that.* Right now Bill had to focus on the current action they were conducting. He looked first to Charlie and then to Ruff. He didn't know what he expected to read in their faces, but saw nothing disturbing. He asked. "How should we approach this? Would you believe, I have never been in this canyon before. I assume that the box end is steep. Ruff, you said you were here once, what do you think? Isn't it too steep for this group to climb?"

"The curbing on the streets of Fort Collins is too steep for some of this group. Those CBI guys are in street shoes for crying out loud. Why didn't someone tell them to wear boots?"

Charlie was grinning ear to ear, listening to Ruff, but he quickly wiped it off when Bill glared at him.

"I didn't think I would have to dress them when I agreed they could come along. They're big boys, let them take care of themselves. Now what do you think about our approach? I'm thinking of sending Captain Russell with one of the squads of Rangers up ahead as a scouting unit. The rest of the 'invasion force,' as I understand it is called by some, can lay back as a reserve group."

Ruff realized that Bill was concerned about what they might find somewhere at the far end of the canyon. He knew his friend carried a huge responsibility. So Ruff decided to play it straight, he didn't want to make it more difficult for his buddy.

Ruff said, "I like your thinking. An advance scout force is a good idea. But I would suggest that you let Charlie and me be that force. Just the two of us. We could make better time and do it without attracting attention to ourselves. I've been watching your Rangers; they're not the quietest people on earth. Plus, don't forget, I left the shotgun man on the creek bank. He knows who I am, I don't think he will feel threatened by an old man. But if a squad of Rangers goes charging into his camp, it could get ugly fast. Charlie and I could approach the box end with less chance of being noticed. Also, if we run into that shotgun, we will seem like less of a threat to the person wielding the weapon."

"I have no authority to place you in harms' way, Ruff. I don't like the idea of you, a civilian, being injured in an official operation. But, you are here, and you and Charlie were the ones to decipher what you think is going on. I tell you what: if you can promise not to take any chances and will back off if you run into trouble, I'll consider it. Remember that we still have to find your nephew, and I need you for that search. And keep this in mind, you're the one who has to answer to Jennifer, not me."

"You're right, Jennie is my responsibility. And I'll take care of her and Mike. She knows that."

Ruff felt a little guilty. He wasn't completely being open with his buddy. Ever since they had found the first set of rocks, he had thought of Mike. He couldn't explain it, and he had no evidence to substantiate his belief, but there was something about those rocks. At first, Ruff thought it was wishful thinking that Mike could be near. But his instinct told him to believe that it was true. Some how, some way, Mike is connected to the trail mark. Ruff just knew it. And if Mike is in this canyon, Ruff planned find him at all costs.

His thoughts faded as he came back to the present and noticed that his friend Bill was studying him. *He can read me every bit as much as I can read him, Ruff thought. I've got to convince him, and the best way to do that is to be truthful with him.*

"Speaking of the search, how's that list of campers coming along, Bill? It's a very short list, isn't it? I know you think that I am hiding something from you. I'm not really; it's just that I have this gut feeling that somehow Mike is involved in this scenario that Charlie and I believe in." Bill started to say something but Ruff kept speaking, "You just said that I had to answer to Jennie, now let me do it, give me a chance to answer to her by sending me with Charlie. You can put him in charge. You can always say I went with him on my own; that I disobeyed you. You can always convince the Park Superintendent of that! Can't you, Bill?" Ruff forced a grin from his friend.

"Okay, okay, I hate to hear an old man beg. But you be careful, and Charlie, you're in charge. Don't for a minute let this old codger forget that."

"Who are you calling an old codger? But thanks, Bill, I'll behave."

"Get out of here before I change my mind. We'll give you two a half-hour head start. Remember that we will be a half-hour behind you, so if you discover anything, anything at all, one, or both of you, hightail it back and keep us informed. You got that Ruff?"

"Yes, daddy, let's go, Charlie."

"Hey, I'm in charge, remember? I say when we go. Now, let's go." The two grabbed their gear and started for the trail down the canyon valley.

Bill let out a soft groan. "I know I am going to live to regret this."

CHAPTER 25

Surveying the interior of the cabin, Mike was exposed to a totally new world. In all the videos, movies, and television programs he had watched, never had he seen any thing like it. The cabin was actually one room. The first thing Mike noticed about the room was the floor. There wasn't one. Dirt made up the floor, packed to a hard shiny surface from long usage. It appeared that water was sprinkled on the floor, and then walked on with bare feet so that in time, the floor developed a hard glassy surface that seldom needed to be swept.

The log sides of the cabin came down to rest on the ground, and mud packing along the edge of the interior and between the logs made up the walls of the cabin. The corner to the left of the cabin door, contained a narrow bed that Mike assumed had to be the sleeping quarters for both Ham and Will, even though it looked barely large enough for one of them. A short rope ran from the cabin wall to a small tree trunk about six feet tall, attached to the bedpost with a short piece of small rope on the side of the bed nearest the cabin door. This appeared to serve as a privacy curtain, for on the bed lay an extra folded blanket. Mike guessed that it could also be used as a second blanket in cold weather.

The bed had no sheets nor did it have pillows, just a thin stained mattress with a hole in it that ran along the bottom edge. A bucket set under the bed, and Mike wondered if it might be a night urinal.

To the right of the cabin door a similar set-up existed with a slightly larger bed, but the mattress had stains and holes in it also. On the bed was one yellowed pillow without a cover and two folded blankets. Again, there was the tree trunk and rope across the side of the bed nearest the door. The only difference Mike could see was the absence of a bucket under the bed. Mike assumed that this sleeping area was for Pap and Emma, because of the presence of the pillow; he also wondered if the pillow went on Emma's side of the bed or of Pap's.

In the center of the room directly in front of the cabin door, was a table about two feet wide and four feet long, made of two slabs of wood. A chunk of wood about three feet high under each end of the slabs, served as table legs. In places, particularly along the edges where the slabs met in the center of the table, there was as much as an inch gap between the slabs. Mike could see crosscut saw marks along the surface of the table.

Along the sides of the table were two chairs per side. The chairs appeared to be factory made, but not one of the chairs matched any of the other three. One had no back to it, and one had a leg that had been replaced by a piece of kindling somehow stuck through the seat of the chair into the piece of kindling. To Mike, it appeared to have been put there through pure force. Mike noticed that there was absolutely nothing on the top of the table. No cover, no salt nor pepper shaker, no sugar bowl, nothing.

Along the cabin wall between the end of the bed and the back cabin wall was another slab similar to the table slabs. This slab was only about a foot from the floor and rested on two chunks of wood that sat on the floor. Placed on the slab was one pot, black on the outside. One could only assume the color came from wood fire smoke. There was one large ladle, encrusted with food particles that Mike guessed were from previous use. Also there were four mismatched deep-dish plates, not stacked, but setting side-by-side along the slab. Two of the plates were badly chipped and one that had a severe crack. All four still had chunks of dried food on them.

Near the center of the back wall was a fireplace made from stones similar to the ones Mike had noticed in the valley of the box canyon. There was no hearth, and no mantle. Only a tripod looking affair that Mike thought resembled the one he had made at the campsite. There was a pot, very similar to the one on the slab, that was being held over a small fire, by the tripod. Mike assumed that whatever was in the pot must be very hot, but he could distinguish neither aroma nor any steam coming from it. There were several short candles, all well used, lying on the floor off to the side.

Beside the candles was an old lantern. It was plain, four glass sides, with a wire handle that Mike guessed was used for hanging the lantern. The glass was greasy and he could barely see what looked like one of the short candles inside. There were no other ornaments around the fireplace. No clothes drying on a rack, no empty cooking vessels, not one additional pot or pan. Just one metal bucket piled high with ashes. Along the fourth wall, in the space between Ham and Will's bed and the back wall of the cabin, was a fourth wood slab. Again, it was about a foot off the floor, held there with chunks of wood. On this slab were various items. The first thing to catch Mike's eye was the two bear hides that Ham and Will had worked so diligently on when Mike was first there. They were folded neatly and stacked one on top of the other, on the slab.

There were several tools lined up along the slab. First, an old double bladed axe, with several nicks in the blade on both cutting edges. It's handle was also badly damaged just inches below the axe head. Mike had been around Ruff long enough to know that someone had missed the target with the axe many times for the handle to be so chewed up at that spot. Second was two large shiny carving knives; one had a wooden handle that appeared to be homemade. Beside those, was a small old hunting knife, the kind of knife a youngster might carry. Mike wondered, *might there have been a third child at one time? Where would they ever put a third child?* Mike guessed that from the look of the knives that they were very sharp. Then there was a space on the slab with nothing. Something was missing: then it came to him, *the corn knife. That's the spot where the corn knife was kept. It must still be at the site of the attack.*

At the near end of the slab, was a pile of old rags. Mike wondered about that, and suddenly realized that they weren't rags at all, they were the extra clothes that the family owned. Looking again, Mike could make out that some of them were Emma's, and some belonged to the boys and Pap. None were folded, and because of the stains and wear and tear of the garments, Mike could not attest to the cleanliness of them either.

When he turned around to face the cabin door, Mike noticed a set of deer antlers spaced door-width apart, above the door: Just the place for the shotgun. It was then he realized that he still carried the weapon. He reached up to put the gun in its spot on the antlers, but he couldn't reach it. He wasn't tall enough! Embarrassed, Mike turned back around and looked at Pap. Without saying a word, Pap stepped forward and took the gun from Mike's hands and placed it in its cradle above the door. He then walked to the table took a chair and motioned for Mike to take the one across from him. Mike did as he was silently told.

Pap turned to Emma and said, "we'ens eat."

*   *   *

A half-hour later the meal was over and Mike was sated. At first he wondered about the plate of food Emma had set before him. It wasn't a very large helping and Mike noticed food remnant leftovers, on the plate. *Is this Ham's or Will's plate?* he asked himself. But by the end of the meal, he had consumed three helpings from the pot on the fire. He had never tasted anything so bland in his life, and he never tasted anything so good. Mike couldn't even remember when he had last eaten. He was so absolutely famished that the unseasoned food tasted great. On the third helping, he tried to determine what he was eating, there were potatoes, turnips, and some sort of bean, but he wasn't sure he wanted to know what else. He knew that he was full and that was all that mattered to him.

It was now mid-morning and when Pap stood from the table, he motioned to Emma. It was only then that she got one of the two remaining plates and served herself. Mike noticed that she took a very small helping. What was it they say about the food when the cook won't eat? By then, Pap had opened the cabin door and stepped out into the bright sun.

Mike followed, but it took him a few minutes for his eyes to adjust to the sunlight. Until then he hadn't realized just how dark it was in the cabin. It dawned on him that the cabin was without windows; the only light came from the small fire. When Mike had been a prisoner earlier at the cabin, he had noticed what little time Emma spent outside of the cabin. How depressing for her that must be; she spent most of every day in the gloomy dark cabin.

Few words passed between them, as Mike and Pap set out with the travois to complete their gruesome job of recovering the bodies of the slain brothers. Since the site of the bear attack wasn't more than a few hundred yards from the cabin, they became aware of the presence of the two slain brothers well before reaching the site itself. Will and Ham were beginning to stink; there was no other way to express it. When they arrived at the site of the bloated bodies, Mike immediately lost much of the meal he had just consumed.

In the clear daylight, the attack on the two was extremely vivid, and much more real than it had been in the semi-darkness of early dawn. Carefully, so as not to cause any damage and thereby increase the odor, they positioned the two brothers on the travois, being extra careful not to lose Ham's head in the process. Nothing but skin and a neck muscle held it to the rest of the body. Soon they were ready to drag the travois to the cabin.

Adjusting the harness to his size, Mike leaned into the pull. The travois did not move. Only when Pap donned his harness and began to pull could they move the travois sufficiently to make any progress. As they toiled in the morning sun, Mike began to wonder what they were going to do with the bodies when they got back to the cabin. There was no way to preserve them, and the stink would only get worse. *I wonder if Pap has thought about that,* mused Mike silently. During one of the many breaks they took while moving the bodies the few hundred yards they had to cover, Mike ventured to ask.

"Pap . . . can I call you Pap; or should I call you something else?"

"Pap fen," he replied.

"Pap, what are we going to do with Ha . . . er, the two boys when we get to the cabin?" Mike started to use their given names, but caught himself in time.

"We'ens got a place fer em, ya sees."

Mike waited for Pap to say more, but when he didn't, Mike decided he would have to just wait and see.

As they arrived at the cabin, Pap motioned for Mike to go to the right. There, practically hidden from sight, was a slab wood door laid atop a wood frame just inches above the ground. The only evidence of its use was the slightly trampled path leading to it. Pap stopped the travois near the structure, released himself from his harness, and pulled open the door. There was a hole in the ground beneath the door.

At first Mike thought of an old root cellar Ruff had showed him on his grandfather's old place, but this was just a hole, no steps leading down into it, no apparent walls, except for the earth itself. The opening itself was about four feet square.

Pap went to the side of the cabin and retrieved a ladder. It appeared to be something that a youngster would have made. It was only about four feet long and made of tree limbs. Rope lashings tied the crosspieces to the vertical legs. Mike wondered if it had ever been used, for it didn't appear to him to be stout enough to support the weight of Pap, or his boys.

Pap dropped one end of the ladder into the hole. The top of the ladder barely reached the door frame. He left it there and went into the cabin. Mike waited; he didn't know what else to do. Shortly, Pap reappeared with the old lantern Mike had noticed earlier. Pap carried the lantern in such a way as to give it protection from the movement as it was lit but gave off very little light. Mike thought that if the glass were cleaned it would illuminate the area around it better. But he decided that was something Pap would find unnecessary.

Pap handed the lantern to Mike, climbed down the ladder easier than Mike would have thought he could, and placed the lantern along the side of the hole in the ground. There were other things in the hole, but Mike could not tell what they were from the bright back lighting of the sun.

After moving some things around in the hole, Pap climbed out, and motioned for Mike to unlash the bodies from the travois. Pap watched as Mike awkwardly tried to do his task without touching the bodies. Pap apparently decided that the boy needed assistance, and pitched in to help. To Mike the stink was getting stronger. He hesitated when Pap motioned for him to go down the ladder first. He started to complain, then thought better of it, and proceeded down into the hole. As he stepped off the ladder, he looked up and Pap was already handing down the first body.

Because the head was hanging well away from the body, Mike could tell it was Ham. He about lost the rest of his last meal, but he managed to keep his stomach under control. Letting the rest of the body to drop on the floor, Mike dragged it away from the ladder. By the time he got to the opening, Pap was already pushing the second body through to him. Mike managed to catch the shoulders of Will so that only the bottom half of the body hit the ground with a loud thud. Mike figured Pap was going to scold him, but Pap said nothing. He started climbing down the ladder.

Stopping for a break from the heavy lifting, Mike looked around the hole. That's all it was: a hole carved out of the earth. He could tell by the rocks in the sides, that some of the excavation had been chiseled out, probably with Emma's pickax, he thought. The hole was empty except for two bundles that Pap had moved to one side. Taking a closer look, Mike could see that they were black bear hides. *Two of them, from the looks of things,* Mike thought, *and it looks like they have been here for a while. If someone finds out about this, Pap would be in a lot of trouble.* About that time, Mike looked up to see Pap doing something he rarely did: he was looking directly into Mike's eyes.

"Wot ya tinkin, boy?" He demanded. Mike hesitated before replying.

"I know what is in the bundles. You could get into trouble for having bear hides in a national forest, you know." Mike figured the best thing to do was to be truthful.

"Ya talk? This one of a deed bar."

"I don't know if that makes a difference or not," Mike answered honestly. "Maybe it does."

In an instant, Pap climbed out of the hole and hurried to the cabin. Mike was puzzled until he saw Pap come back out the door with the two bundles of cub hide. He walked to the hole where Mike stood and dropped them both at Mike's feet. Climbing back into the hole, he grabbed both bundles and placed them with the others. Turning to Mike he said simply, "thay's be safer down here, then in the cabin." The two stood for a few minutes looking at each other, Pap not talking and Mike not knowing what to say. Finally Pap shrugged his shoulders and spoke with no emotion visible in his voice.

"We'ens best be gittin out a 'ear, boy. Et be gittin stout en air shortly." With the strength of a much younger man, Pap dragged the two bodies as far into the hole as he could. Then, without looking at Mike, climbed the ladder and was out of the hole. Pap turned and looked at Mike, still standing in the hole. For a minute, Mike thought he was going to be left there. But Pap leaned down and offered his hand. Mike hesitated only for a second, then took the old man's hand. Pap pulled him up. Pap, with a fluid motion, retrieved the ladder with one hand and closed the door on the hole with the other.

Going to the cabin, he picked up the shovel once more, and walked back to the door of the hole, where he proceeded to shovel dirt upon all the cracks in the wood. Only when he was finally satisfied that the odor from the bodies was contained, did he stop shoveling. Then he turned to Mike and said, "Ya best git, boy"

"But you'll need a witness, someone to tell the auth . . . Marshall what happened."

"We'ens don't wont ya ta git in tro'ble wit em. Understand, boy?"

"But . . ." Mike was out of words.

"Best ya git, boy. I's 'preciate ya corn'cern." Pap dropped the shovel near the door and opening it, went inside, closing the door behind him. Almost immediately the door re-opened and Emma stepped out. She had an old gray cloth that was gathered into a ball. Handing Mike the cloth, she patted his forearm and retreated back inside, closing the door behind her. Mike opened one corner of the cloth and found that Emma had put four small boiled potatoes inside. Mike stood for a long time hoping the door would open once again. As Mike stood there alone, he thought about the potatoes. Would Emma have to explain the loss of four small potatoes? Not wanting to get her in trouble he started to go to the door and insist she take them back. Then he realized that he might be slapping her generosity in the face if he did.

Instead, he went to the water well and dropped the bucket into it. When he pulled the bucket out, Mike took a long drink and then filled his water bottle, which still hung on his belt. Resigning himself to the fact that he had been dismissed as if a child, Mike finally dropped his shoulders in surrender. He turned away from the cabin door, hardly noticing that the sun had traveled well past its apex in the western sky. Looking like a lost pup, Mike slowly begin to make his way down the valley trail.

CHAPTER 26

Charlie had been quiet during the conversation between Bill and Ruff. But there was something that had been said by Ruff that bothered him and he wasn't sure why. So, after a few minutes of quietly climbing up the valley trail, he asked Ruff the question that was on his mind.

"Ruff, what did you mean by that statement you made to Bill?"

"What statement?"

"The one about Mike somehow being involved in this valley expedition."

"It's just a feeling I have. You know, like the ache you get in the pit of your stomach? The one that tells you something doesn't fit, or something isn't right? I know that in this line of work, you've probably had that feeling before."

"Okay, I'll give you that, but tell me, what doesn't 'fit'? What doesn't seem right to you?"

"Charlie, you have been reading sign in the forest for some time now, don't tell me that you don't have some question about the trail markers we found the day before yesterday."

"What was I supposed to read into them? We agreed they were crudely done and poorly placed."

"That's just my point. You and I both know that whoever placed the markers was not a wilderness-savvy person. An amateur who had either heard about it or read it in a book placed them-not someone who had actually practiced marking a trail."

"So that means . . . ?" Charlie followed Ruff's thinking, but he wanted to give him a chance to finish his thoughts.

"You know what that means. How many hikers did Bill tell you were unaccounted for by this district? One or two? You know that Mike is probably the only misplaced camper that is out on the trail somewhere.

Mike made those markers and he's in this canyon someplace. I just know it."

"Okay, lets say you're right—Mike is one of the parties that we are trailing. Which one? The one being pursued, or the one stalking?"

"That's what is puzzling to me. If he is being pursued, why? And by whom? If he is doing the stalking, why? And whom is he stalking? That's what worries me, and puzzles me. That's what I want from you, I want to know what you're thinking."

"You're asking a lot from a kid from Chicago."

"I'm not asking a kid from Chicago, I'm asking the best tracker in the Canyon Lakes Division of the Colorado Rangers."

"Well, now that you put it that way, I'll give you my best-educated Colorado Ranger answer: I haven't the foggiest idea. You know Mike better than I do, what do you think? If Mike is leading, does he know where he is going? If he is stalking, then is he trying to find something? You tell me, Ruff, what is in Mike's head?"

By this time, the two entered an open clearing devoid of trees. Knowing that they needed to leave some sort of trail mark for the contingent of law enforcement officials following them, Charlie found a rock pile that he would not have to disturb in order to arrange a marker, he simply had added to it. Someone specifically looking for it would spot it, but would not attract the attention of others traveling the same trail.

While Charlie set about the task of leaving a trail mark, Ruff was mulling over in his mind the questions that Charlie had posed to him. *Charlie is right, I need to get inside Mike's head. What is he thinking and why? Which party was Mike, and which party wasn't? If Mike is the one leaving the trail mark, why? If he is the one being stalked, why? And more importantly, does Mike know he is being stalked?*

Ruff knew that to get anywhere in his thinking, he had to make some choices. *What was it that he always told his audience when making a lecture,—"trust your instincts." So, Ruff, do as you preach, trust your instincts, and let your gut lead you.*

Catching up with Charlie as he finished the marker, Charlie and Ruff headed down the trail. Ruff slapped him on the shoulder.

"Okay, here's what I think," Ruff said. Charlie turned to listen.

"I have Mike following, doing the stalking. Why? Maybe because he thinks that whoever he is following can somehow help him. Remember that he doesn't know the territory and is basically lost. Maybe he thinks those whom he is following know where they're going. Mike needs to find me. He knows Bill and he knows Bill can find me. So he could be trying to locate someone who can lead him to Bill."

Charlie raised his hand as if in a classroom. "One question. Why is he following so secretly that he is trying to leave trail markers? Why isn't he with the other party?"

Ruff stared at his friend. With an exasperated look on his face, Ruff paused then finally spoke.

"I'm not sure, but the other party must appear to him as some sort of threat. He doesn't trust them for some reason, so he is marking the trail for himself. So he can follow it back."

"Back to where?" Charlie said. Ruff again gave his friend a hard stare for several seconds. He decided Charlie wasn't trying to be difficult and answered as best he could.

"You don't fool me, Chicago boy, not for a minute. I know you are trying to get me to fine-tune my thinking and you're doing a good job of that." Ruff chuckled, and with a slight smirk on his face, continued. "As for what is in Mike's head, I can only speculate. But I think there is only one location he can identify with, and that is the campsite we set up on the Cache La Poudre tributary. If he is pulling up skills he has learned from my many lectures, and I believe he is, the campsite is his home base, the place he would return to as a reference point."

"So you think Mike is using you as a reference to decide what he should do?"

"I think the boy is using his own skills. They may be a little amateurish, but they're being implemented by reactions to his environment. He is thinking like a wilderness camper," said Ruff, his face taking on a glow of pride and satisfaction. If he proved to be right in his assumptions of what was happening on the trail, he felt that Mike could fast be coming into his own as a man of nature.

Charlie wasn't finished yet. "If you are right in who the stalking party is, and we don't really know that it is Mike, and you are right that he mistrusts the folks he is trailing, then why take the risk? Why is he staying on their trail when he has a fear of them? There has to be a reason for him to continue to track them."

"As I said before, he sees them as an aid. A solution to the problem not knowing what his location is. If a person doesn't know where they are, then that person doesn't know where he is going, right? And I think Mike has figured that out on his own. He knows that he has to determine that first. That's what I meant when I said he was thinking like a wilderness man."

"Then if you're right, Mike is in control, unless those he is following decide to take action against him. That threat you mentioned. If they threaten him, he could be in serious trouble. We have no idea who it is he is following, if you're thinking is correct, I am a little concerned for his safety." As he spoke, he noticed the change that came over Ruff's face, and knew in an instant that Ruff felt the same concern, only many times over.

"I can't help but think that those three I ran into are the same ones that Mike is following. Somehow, somewhere, Mike and those three have crossed paths. They had little fear of me, they would have no fear of Mike, but my nephew could, and probably would have a fear of them. I think they fit the mold of the type of people we are talking about when we describe those Mike is trailing. This could be a dangerous game Mike is playing. Deadly dangerous."

Ruff finished his thoughts with a grim look on his face. Charlie's face was just as grim.

CHAPTER 27

Weariness rapidly overcame Mike's determination to locate the small stream that was beside the site of his camp. Mike suddenly realized that he had slept very little in the last forty-eight hours. With the sun setting and his exhaustion, lack of sleep was rapidly catching up with him.

He started looking on both sides of the valley trail for something, anything, that would offer him shelter. *As long as I am in the box canyon I can't get lost. All I have to do is follow this trail. The tricky part is when I leave the canyon, then I will have to rely on my trail markers to help me find my way back to the campsite.* Mike slowly moved down the trail when he suddenly spotted something. *There! By that little bush. Is that what I think it is? A cave?*

Mike left the trail and climbed up the steep slope of the canyon. Upon closer inspection, Mike found that indeed it was a cave and a large one at that. Much bigger than the indentation where he had camped a couple of days ago. It appeared to be about ten to fifteen feet deep, with a ceiling of about six feet. Using his hunting knife, he cut some pine boughs and rigged up a bed for himself about five feet inside the cave. Then he arranged some of the brush from the surrounding area, and hid the cave opening as best he could.

Someone with sharp eyes could still see a little bit of the opening, but maybe this will hide it enough so that no one will investigate. After all, in a few hours it will be dark anyway. I guess I can afford to eat some of the potatoes that Emma gave me. I don't have any thing to go with them except these few berries that I found in the process of covering the cave opening with the bushes. Mike consumed two of the potatoes and a handful of berries. He took two short pulls on his water bottle.

Crawling onto the pine bough bed he had fashioned, he squirmed around until he was satisfied with how it felt. He thought how lucky he was to have found the cave. He let his mind drift through the day's events: the attack of the bear, the death of Will and Ham, the compassion shown by both Pap and Emma, the retrieving of the two boys, and their burial in the root cellar, and the depressive interior of the cabin. It all seemed so surreal to Mike, almost like a fantasy. As his mind relaxed, so did his body, and soon he fell fast asleep. The potatoes and berries did their job, as his body was satisfied with food, and because of the contentment, this sleep would be a deep sleep. A sleep that could cost him dearly if lady luck played out her vile hand against him. Would good luck forsake him now, when he needed it the most?

*   *   *

Ruff looked at the steep sidewall of the canyon and noticed the strange configuration about halfway up. He pulled his attention away from it when he checked the location of the sun, fast disappearing behind the same steep side of the canyon wall. It concerned Ruff that they had not made better time traversing the length of the box canyon. For some reason, and he wasn't sure what the reason may have been, it had taken the main body of the "invasion force" considerable time to make it to the rendezvous point. Bill and Charlie had settled on a clearing along the steep rocky face of the canyon, for the meeting spot, when Charlie and Ruff were sent ahead to scout out the interior of the large canyon.

Ruff's gaze fell once again on the place halfway up the canyon wall. Nothing appeared out of the ordinary about the spot, and that was what bothered Ruff; it seemed a little too ordinary for him. He mentioned his thoughts to Charlie, who was busy with the radio, trying to make contact with Bill and the rest of the "invasion force." Charlie dismissed Ruff's attempt to call his attention to the location on the canyon wall. Ruff had no real concern with the spot and with Charlie's nonchalant attitude toward it, Ruff let it go and concentrated on what Charlie was saying into the radio:

"Yes, sir. We can just make it out from here. About a half-mile in front of where Ruff and I are right now, there is a clearing along the trail, with plenty of open space for a campsite. We could bivouac there for the night and be fresh and ready for the box end of the canyon in the morning."

Bill must have acknowledged Charlie's suggestion, as the ranger nodded his head several times as if Bill could see his head move. Then after listening to the radio for a few more minutes, Charlie said, "I understand, we should have traversed the canyon in a day, but you have a group of officials with you that were not prepared for this type of terrain and are not used to traveling through the woods of a national forest. Yes, sir, but it's not your fault, I heard you give the CBI your instructions. You told them what to expect. Don't hold yourself responsible for their shortcomings." Charlie again listened. He closed out the conversation, saying,.

"Yes sir, we will meet you on the trail. The clearing is about a half-mile for us and about a mile and a quarter for you. Yes, sir, we will check for water in the vicinity, but just in case, tell your people to save their water. That's not good, sir, they should be more conservative of their water. Yes, sir, see you in about one hour."

"One hour! One hour to travel one mile? What kind of wusses do we have following us anyway! It's been this way all day!" When Charlie disconnected with the radio, Ruff ranted on, but Charlie's thoughts were on business.

"Never mind that now. Let's just get on down the trail and see if we can find water for that group. Bill says that some of them have been complaining about not having anything to drink for the past hour. They'll be hurting by morning, for sure."

"Serves them right," muttered Ruff, "they must be drinking the stuff like fish. I tell you; if I were in charge the fur would be flying. Why I'd . . ."

Ruff suddenly realized he was probably criticizing his good friend Bill, and his efforts to manage the composite and unprepared group Ruff was haranguing. He glanced at Charlie, who was grinning from ear to ear and he became even more livid—so much so, that he couldn't think of anything more to say. All he could do was growl, "Let's get going and find that water."

Ruff was so preoccupied that he started marching up the canyon trail and put aside his thoughts about the place on the side of the canyon wall. But during the evening hours that night, Ruff's thoughts returned to the spot. "Charlie let's check out that ledge, I've got a feeling I need to satisfy." But being a more practical thinker, Charlie vetoed the idea.

"There is no moon, and therefore no light to find our way. It would be a waste of time and effort. Forget about it Ruff, and get some rest. We don't know what we will find tomorrow at the box end of the canyon. We might need all the energy we can muster."

"I suppose you're right again." Ruff replied gruffly, "but still I would like to check it out. Maybe we can do that on the way back to the mouth of the canyon." Charlie gave a short nod.

CHAPTER 28

Halfway across the morning sky, the sun's rays were just clipping the closed eyelids of Mike's face. He jerked awake. Standing he realized this would be one of those times when his head was wide-awake, but his body would still be half-asleep. His stiff muscles and his joints ached. But his mind was alert and refreshed from a full night of sleep. From the way his body felt he decided that his makeshift bed had not been so comfortable as he had thought. But he was ready to move. As he exited the cave he noticed several paw prints around the entrance. The tracks disappeared as they led down the steep rock face of the canyon wall. *I must have had a visitor last night,* he thought, *those look fresh. Wow, a bear outside and me trapped in the cave. I wonder why the bear didn't bother me? Why did it just ignore me? It must have known that I was in the cave. Lady luck, you must still be with me!*

Mike adjusted his meager belongings about him. He noticed the open clearing that he had crossed in the late afternoon the day before. It still looked the same, deserted. He turned and started down the valley following the trail. Mike noticed that the trail looked a little more worn than yesterday, but thought little about it. He was anxious to reach the open end of the box canyon and see if his trail markers were still in place. And he was doubly excited about reaching the campsite along the river. He anticipated eating a big meal from the food still secreted there. At least, he hoped it was still there and no varmint had gotten into it.

As he hiked along the trail, Mike's mind wandered back to the cabin. *What will Pap do now that his boys are gone? Will he return home? Where is home to him and Emma, anyway? Maybe he is home! I bet he lives in the forest and doesn't have anywhere else to go. What if the authorities, or as Emma calls him, the Marshall, found them? What would happen? If the Marshall found the bear hides in the cabin and in the hole, they would surly charge him with some sort of poaching law. Would they send him to jail? I wouldn't like that, being locked up in a cage. I bet Pap would go bananas in jail.*

Because he was refreshed and sure of the route he was taking, Mike made good time in getting to the mouth of the canyon. There he found his first marked tree and turned in the direction it pointed out for him to go. After traveling some one hundred yards, he searched for another marked tree and located it with little trouble. He knew that the next marker should be a rock pile pointing him in a different direction.

After hiking the distance that he guessed would get him to the next marker, he was faced with a problem: he couldn't find the rock pile that he thought should be there. Spending a quarter of an hour looking, he finally gave up and checked his bearings with the little compass on the magnifying glass. Quickly finding north, he turned around. Hiking eagerly, as if he had something to prove, he angled off in the opposite direction, positive he knew the direction to go and find the river.

Mike's dead reckoning was somewhat accurate, for after traveling about one hundred and fifty yards; he soon found another tree with a mark near the bottom of it. The mark pointed him towards the proper direction. *I guess I remember more than I thought I would, when I made the marks.* Mike was proud of his ability to find his way in the woods. *I wonder if Ruff would be as pleased as I am* he mused to himself. Luck, skill, what ever someone wanted to call it, Mike felt pride in himself.

By evening light he was following the little stream down river knowing the campsite lay just a little way further. He had traveled the distance in about a day, nearly the same amount of time that it had taken him to trail the three from the campsite to the cabin several days ago. Mike was tired but extremely proud of his accomplishment. He set about inspecting the camp and searching for the food cache that he and Ruff had stashed; it seemed a lifetime ago.

*   *   *

Captain Russell had aroused the "invasion force" at daybreak. It took him little time to roust his rangers, but after several tries to awaken the others, he started using a prod made from a sharpened tree branch. The sharp pointed instrument did its job, they were soon awake. The CBI guys and the Highway Patrol troopers were easily awakened also. The night before, about a quarter of a mile to the left of the trail, Charlie had been fortunate in finding a small stream. The first thing some of the men did upon arising, was visit the stream, and using purification tablets distributed by Captain Russell, fill their canteens. Feeling a bit of responsibility he warned them about consuming the water before the tablets had a chance to do their work.

"We'll eat a cold breakfast and be on the trail in twenty minutes," Bill Waddle announced to the group. "Anybody not ready will be left behind. So get a move on."

Charlie and Ruff stood with Captain Russell at the edge of the clearing. They were watching Sheriff Crocker open a can of dog food. He was having a great deal of trouble with the opener. After finally succeeding in his task, he casually tossed the empty can among the bushes. Captain Russell responded quickly, and he did so with more than a little bit of authority in his voice.

"Hey Sheriff, pick up that can and carry it out of the forest with you. We don't litter the park with debris, no matter who we are."

The Sheriff grumbled something under his breath, but picked up the can.

"Here goes twenty minutes of daylight down the drain. And we'll still have some guys with their shoes untied when we start." The other two didn't respond to Ruff's assessment of the situation, however, if a vote of the accuracy of his statement had been taken, it probably would have passed unanimously. True to his word, Bill ordered the rangers to move out twenty minutes later. The sheriff, last to fall in line, hurriedly laced up his boots while trying to corral his dog, when Bill gave the order. Exchanging a look with Ruff, the district superintendent smiled and simply stated, "At least he has boots on."

Another hour passed before the roughly constructed cabin came into view. Immediately, Bill halted the unit. Leaving the main force just out of sight from the cabin, he gave them instructions to remain quiet and stay put. He told them he didn't want anyone doing anything unless they had direct orders from him.

"And put a muzzle on that dog, Sheriff, I don't want him making a ruckus."

With that, he and Captain Russell, along with Charlie and Ruff, approached the cabin cautiously. They could detect no life about the place.

"It looks deserted," the Captain said quietly.

"Hard to tell, though I don't see any smoke coming from the fire place flue," answered Bill.

"I supposed we could go to the door and knock." Ruff said, half joking.

"Let's just go as far as the well, I'll call out to the cabin from there. You guys be ready for anything but no one fires a weapon unless fired upon. Is that clear?" Everyone nodded their heads in unison.

Bill, followed by the others, reached the water well and called out.

"Hello, the cabin. This is Roosevelt District Superintendent Bill Waddle; I would like to talk to you." Bill's call met with silence.

"Sir let me do what Ruff suggested, knock on the door. If we don't get a response from the person, or persons illegally occupying a structure on federal land, then we have the authority under both Colorado law, and under the National Park Federal Guidelines, to enter the premises and conduct a legal search of the area."

Bill gazed at Captain Russell and realized that he was not the one who should be calling the shots. This was really the Captain's operation, and protocol called for him to lead the action. Bill needed to allow Russell the opportunity to conduct the maneuver with the authority his position dictated. Bill nodded to Captain Russell.

Adjusting his equipment belt on his hips, the Captain slowly approached the cabin door and knocked.

CHAPTER 29

With the sun setting low in the sky, Mike knew he was out of luck in starting a fire with the use of his magnifying glass. Necessity dictated that he take another approach, so Mike began a search through one of the camp packs for the matches he knew were there. He finally found what he was looking for and with the aid of some tissue paper, soon had a good fire going in the fire pit. He could hear the comment his uncle would have made: "Not exactly the way a wilderness man would have started the fire, but it got the job done." Grinning at his own humor, he set about to boil some water for drinking and cooking purposes.

After a trip to the stream with the small iron kettle and putting a pot of water on the tripod, he started rummaging through the packs for something to eat. He found what he wanted, a package of pancake mix and a can of sausage gravy. Sausage gravy on freshly cooked pancakes was one of his favorites. *He could see his mother's facial expression now. With her nose turned up and with gritted teeth, she would frown at the thought of his devouring three or four eight-inch pancakes covered with thick sausage gravy. Too bad I don't have some real sausage to crumble up in the gravy,* he reflected with a smile.

After finishing what was to him a filling, and delicious meal, Mike decided to square away his campsite. One thing he noticed about the tent, it had accumulated dust and debris from the wind and a few crawly bugs had set up housekeeping in it also, removing the pegs, he gave it a good shake. Then he arranged his sleeping bag so that he could look out of the tent and check on the fire pit.

Fortunately, he remembered to repack the food pack with the bear-proof seal, and hoist it high off the ground with the rope apparatus that Ruff had set up the first night they were in camp. *The first night. The only night.* It dawned on Mike that he had not seen Ruff since he went to sleep the first night. *What could have possibly happened to him that night?*

Mike knew Ruff was a responsible person and that he would never allow Mike to be placed in a dangerous situation, but that is exactly what had happened. *And Ruff did not do what he promised to do—To see that nothing bad happened to me. He had promised my mother! His own sister! Ruff, how could you do this? Where are you?*

When Mike realized what he was thinking, he became ashamed. *What's going on with this feeling of being so incapable and unable to care for myself. Why be so down on myself about my own well being? Who said Mike can't take care of himself. No one needs Ruff as a baby sitter. I can do it on my own! I'll show both my mother and Ruff. Mike Anderson can be the wilderness man that Ruff is always talking about. They'll see me do it, and do it well.*

With renewed confidence, Mike set about collecting firewood. That chore completed, he walked to the creek and refilled the pot to boil more water. He had purification tablets in the camp pack, but he liked the idea of boiling the water, then straining it through a cotton cloth. It has to be a better process, he convinced himself, than adding chemicals to the water.

With the campsite in order and all his chores completed, Mike sat for some time just staring into the fire. *What is it about a fire that makes one contemplate his circumstances and life in particular? he wondered.* He began to feel the effects of the day's activity. After stoking the fire, he then crawled into the tent for the second consecutive good night's sleep.

Awakening with just a hint of daylight, Mike first tended the fire. Finding a few burning embers in the fire pit, he set about to find some of the fine "tender," as Ruff called it, from the inside of the tree bark. Using this to ignite the embers left over from the previous night's fire, he soon had a hot, but not too big, of a fire going in the pit. He went to the creek to fill the kettle with water.

After filling the pot with water, he swung around to return to the warmth of his fire. As his glance fell on a small sandy spot along the creek, his eyes widened. There in front of him was a footprint,. or more accurately, a paw print. Mike's amateur eyes could not tell if the print was fresh or not, but he didn't want to take a chance being away from his fire if there was a bear nosing about. Hefting the full pot, he quickly retreated from the streambed. Returning to the fire, he placed the kettle on the tripod, and examined the area between the camp and the creek.

After some time, he decided it was safe to prepare his breakfast. Grabbing the end of the rope tied to a tree, he proceeded to lower the food pack. He found a breakfast food packet that he thought would satisfy him and placed it in the water. Making sure the double seal was in place, he raised the food pack back to its position high above the ground. While his breakfast cooked, he collected some wood for the fire, keeping a sharp eye out for any unwarranted visitors. As he waited silently by the fire, a thrashing sound suddenly came from the area of the creek. It sounded as though someone was coming through the brush. Only this someone was big, black, and growling like it were dealing with a bad day at the office. When the bear came into view, Mike almost fainted. He knew at once that the bear was no stranger. By now she had a familiar way about her walk, but the telling clue was the enormous slash across her face. This is the same bear.

What in the world? How can this be? I can't believe this bear has traveled all the way from the cabin to this particular campsite. Is she following me? Or is the mother in her still looking for her cubs? Mike remembered what worked for him the last time and reached for a large firebrand and snatching it from the fire pit, he made himself as tall as he could, and at the same time held his arms away from his sides to make himself look wider. He recalled one of Ruff's lectures: *When facing a bear, make your self as large as you can. Let the bear question if he wants to tackle something as big as you look.*

The old she-bear stopped at Mike's action. She snorted a couple of times and stomped the ground with her right paw. But, to Mike's surprise, she made no move toward him. Instead, she actually skirted the campsite, giving the area where Mike stood a wide berth. *She doesn't want anything to do with me,* Mike thought, *she doesn't trust me and knows that a human can be dangerous. That wound from Ham's corn knife must still pain her a lot.*

As the old sow disappeared into the brush along the stream, Mike returned the firebrand to the fire pit. He watched the area where she had vanished. He half-expected her to re-appear almost any time, but after several minutes, and no sounds came from the brush, he decided she had moved on. Mike was glad he had replaced the double seal on the food pack and returned it to the position high off the ground. Still a little on edge, Mike fussed with the fire, and eventually considered it safe to open the food packet that was still in the steaming water on the tripod over the fire.

Mike spent the rest of the morning staying close to the fire. He was jittery and jumped at any little noise came from his surroundings. As the sun peeked from behind scattered clouds directly overhead, Mike decided to give the clothes that were worn when Pap forced him to carry the cub pelt, a good soap and rinse in the stream. That done he changed into a clean shirt and jeans. Returning to the stream, and washing the clothes just removed, the busy camper strung the clean clothes on a line stretched between two trees as best as could be done, under the circumstances. *I wonder what Mom would think of my washing my clothes in a stream? Especially since I don't know how to operate the washer in the house.*

Busy around the campsite, the fears subsided and his mind became more relaxed. After a noon meal, he retreated to the tent with the book that had been started the second day of the campout. Instead of opening the book, Mike allowed his thoughts to return to the encounter with the bear that morning, plus the disappearance of Ruff, and the feeling of being a cast-a-way on a deserted island, in addition to his first encounter with the black bear. Soon his thoughts returned to Ruff, and they ended the same way as before. *Where did Ruff go? What has happened to him? And why doesn't he return?* But this time Mike added questions that now seemed to strike with more fear in his heart when his thoughts returned. Hating himself for asking the questions, they came out anyway. *What do I do now? How do I get out of here?*

CHAPTER 30

Captain Russell had his hand on the butt of his sidearm, but had not unlatched the cover on his holster, as the cabin door slowly opened. A small extremely thin woman, dressed in a tattered, ill-fitting black dress peered out of the partially open door. She wore no shoes and her feet appeared to be very calloused. When she did not speak, Captain Russell took the initiative.

"May I ask who you are?"

"I's Emma."

"Emma, is there anyone else in the cabin?"

"Ya wont ta know?"

"I am Captain Russell. I'm with the Colorado Forest Rangers, stationed here in Roosevelt."

"Ya the Mashell?"

"No, I am a captain. Captain Russell. I'm with . . ."

"Ya the Mashell. I's know ya 'ear."

Ed Russell noticed that the woman wore her hair cut quite short, and straight; a style he thought made for easier care. It didn't look like a comb had been near it in some time. Her face, though not unattractive, was quite plain and completely free of any make-up. He wondered about the black dress. Could she in mourning? It was certainly not an everyday work dress. Plus, not only that, it appeared to be about two sizes too large. These observations took a mere matter of seconds. He soon realized that he wasn't making much progress, but he wanted to keep the conversation on a non-confrontational level. He didn't want the lady to decide to clam up and not talk to him.

"Okay, I'm the Marshall, so would you please tell me if there is anyone else in the cabin?"

"No."

"No, what? No, there is no one else in the cabin? Or no, you are not going tell me?"

"Ya best be addlin I's braen, I's the onlest one 'ear."

"May I come in and verify that there is no one else here?"

"Wot ya meen var'fy? I's done tote ya 'ear none 'ear xcept we'ens."

Standing a few feet behind the Captain, Charlie, Ruff and Bill were beginning to find it hard to keep from laughing out loud. They found the conversation hilarious, and were about to burst at the seams. But Captain Edward Russell did not find it funny; he was becoming frustrated to the point of losing it entirely, yet his demeanor remained calm, but firm.

"Emma, let me ask you one more time, can I come into the cabin?"

"Ya ken." And with that she swung the cabin door wide open. The ranger shielded his eyes from the bright sunlight and peered in the cabin. It was immediately clear to him that he could see very little by standing in the doorway of the small structure. He motioned for Charlie to advance. Obeying the silent command, Ranger First Class Charles Jones approached the doorway. The urgency in the face of the Captain, told Charlie there was no humor to the situation. The Captain's manner had changed, the relaxed, and stress-free operation suddenly took on an official and formal direction.

Bill made no move to interfere with Captain Russell's authority. He had given the command over to the Captain and had no intention of revoking it. In addition, the Captain was in uniform, Bill was wearing cameos. He thought it best to let the uniform talk. He noticed the change in the Captain, and wondered if he had picked up on something. He fully trusted both the Captain and his instincts.

The change did not get lost on Ruff either. Standing only a few feet behind the Captain, he could read the transformation that came over Ed Russell. The Captain stood a little straighter and his posture displayed an attitude of alertness that had been missing on the march to the cabin. Ruff also noticed that Russell's eyes were taking in more of their peripheral vision, they were reading the area like scanning a picture. Ruff noticed that Charlie followed suit when the captain unlatched the cover of the holster containing his sidearm. The atmosphere of the situation had changed. The voice had tensed and the Captain's behavior had taken on a seriousness that goes with the threat of danger. Ruff wondered what the Captain sensed at the door of the cabin. Whatever happened, Ruff knew that this man was in charge. The "invasion force" no longer appeared as a joke to Ruff, it took on a reality.,

"Ranger Jones, I want you to station a guard, armed and ready, outside the door of the cabin. Have first squad inspect and secure the out buildings, and then position themselves along the area in front and back of the cabin. Tell Corporal Brooks that he's in charge of second squad, and he's to notify you immediately of anything the squad finds that will tell us what is going down here. Then have the second squad create a protective shield along the perimeter of the clearing, all the way to the surrounding tree line. Give me two of your best men from your squad to go into the cabin with me to conduct a search. I want to know who is inhabiting this place, and why. Remind everyone of the Superintendent's orders, no one is to fire their weapon unless fired upon. Now, get on with it, Charlie, I want those two men standing beside me five minutes ago."

When Captain Russell stepped into the cabin, he did so with a giant stride, wanting to allow space for the two armed flanking rangers on each side of him to have room to enter at the same split second. He was startled at first, as with his great step he bumped into a chair placed at a table that was too close to the door entrance. All three of the men were suddenly thrown into darkness. It took their eyes a few seconds to adjust. The fire in the pit at the back of the cabin was so low as to offer very little light. And the bright sunlight they had just left behind caused their pupils to react to the dark interior very slowly. Captain Russell once again instinctively placed his hand on the butt of his sidearm, only this time the cover was open.

Gradually their vision returned and the three surveyed the cabin's interior. They could observe the entire cabin with one sweep of their eyes. The woman Emma was apparently telling the truth—there appeared to be no one else in the cabin.

Turning to his right, the Captain said "Ranger, see if you can find something to make some light, there at the fireplace."

Captain Russell, with one ranger by his side, waited patiently as the other ranger rifled through the meager collection at the fire hearth. Finally he found a candle lantern that put out a little light when he held it to an ember from the small fire. Handing it to the Captain, he began to build a better fire with the few pieces of kindling available. Between the two sources of light, the interior of the cabin slowly came into view.

There wasn't much to observe however; they were awed by the crudeness of their surroundings.

"Well, at least there is nothing here to indicate any criminal activity." Captain Russell had barely finished his sentence when Charlie stuck his head in the cabin door.

"Captain, we have a problem. There's something you will want to see."

"What is it? I haven't finished in here yet. Can't it wait a few more minutes?"

"I think it has waited a little too long already. We've found some bodies. Human bodies."

CHAPTER 31

Having no idea on the concept of words, the old sow knew nothing about the word instinct, but she certainly knew of her urges and desires. The strongest, and usually the one with the highest priority, would be the urge to eat. Food to her meant anything she could catch, reach, or find. She wasn't particular, and would eat almost anything. Large or small, dead or alive, it didn't make any difference to her. Anything, whether it flew, swam, crawled, or walked was in her range of edible items. She searched for food now. As usual, she always dealt with the urge of a need to eat.

She knew that her cubs were no longer with her, but the why seemed to be lost. As her instincts about where food could be found began to fade, her mind wandered back to her experience on the hill beside the cabin in the box canyon. She knew the place well, even if it was not in her home territory, she often traveled throughout the neighboring territory for it usually provided something to eat. On occasion, some animal parts were dumped in the trees near the cabin, easy food. Had she worried about their origin, she might have put some connection between the humans living in the cabin and the animal body parts found nearby. But her usual instincts dealt only with the devouring of the food and not worry about why it was there.

The recent bout with confusion came from why she had detected the scent of one of her cubs on the hill. For when she investigated the area, all she found were humans occupying the same spot. She swatted the one human with one quick swing of her good paw and it disappeared. When attacked by the other human, she had dealt with it as well. But somewhere in the recesses of her brain she had learned to try to avoid them except when food could be found. The human had hurt her. Humans were scary, but usually easy to deal with. She had made encounters many times before, but she never worried about why she reacts certain ways only that she does. Most of the time she tries to stay out of the way of humans. It didn't occur to her to wonder why she felt so uneasy when they were around. She usually gave little notice to the problem of convincing them to back off. She could relate with the problems experienced when confronting the members of her own species in a neighboring territory. She knew the old sow that lives in the area of the high country just across from the creek. Usually the sow in that territory could be quite difficult to get along with. But her urge for food outweighed any concern about confrontation. She had no understanding that the sow of that territory had the same urge to find and devour food as she did.

The scent of one of my cubs came and there were no holding back the behavior that came over me. There is no why or why not, only a desire, a need to protect my cubs. Something told me that my cubs were on that hill. They were no where in sight but their scent was present. Every effort was made to defend them, but the human hurt me bad. A great pain appeared on my nose and face. The worst part of the encounter is that though there was scent, nothing from sight nor sound occurred to indicate my cubs were there. Why my cubs did not show—there is no understanding, but for my own protection, something told me to leave quickly. My face and nose hurt so much that my desire for food was interrupted for several hours. My face still pains me but it feels much better than it did, but there are a lot of bugs around. They bother me for some reason. They seem to want to live on the place where the human hurt me.

My cub's scent came to me again in the high country where food could also be found. It was near a hole in the wall that sometimes had been used for a deep sleep. But it seemed to be an old scent and so faint that food seemed to be more important to me. Plus there seemed to be a human scent connected to it. Again, something came over me and fleeing from human scent was my reaction. The loss of my cubs wasn't nearly as painful as my face and nose had been. Not being interested in having to deal with another human after the pain suffered from the last one seemed to be the right choice at the time. Leaving the high country and returning to my territory here by the stream, seemed important to me, but now, the humans have returned here also. Why don't they stay away? They are nothing but trouble.

Well, that's not always true, sometimes they can be a good source of food. And much of their food is so wonderfully sweet. My desire for food is increasing just thinking about those round things with the hole in the middle that were found in that knap sack taken from the camping area down the creek just last month. Those things were covered with sugar. There were others in the pack that had a sweet berry taste hidden inside them. That food was almost as good as the honey tree that was found last spring just up river from here.

Now this other human is camping nearby, but he is so scary. He looks big. Don't really want to tangle with him. Besides, there never is any food at his camp. One of my cubs found evidence of food the first time we visited him but nothing else could be detected around. Then he got a piece of that fire and stood up, he looked like he could hurt me. Just this morning came the urge to start looking for some of those delicious green plants and without any reason, he jumped up and became so scary that my reflex was to leave. He is still there, but my past encounters say wait until he puts out that fire. Then maybe there will be something to eat when he isn't watching so closely.

CHAPTER 32

Following behind Charlie, Captain Russell exited the dark and entered the bright sunlight. Standing just outside the doorway for a minute to let his eyes adjust.

"Wait a minute, Charlie, I got to let my eyes soak up some of this daylight." Charlie stopped at the corner of the cabin and glanced back to the Captain. "Sorry, Captain, I was thinking about what I have to show you."

The Captain caught up with Charlie and motioned for him to lead on to wherever he was going. Charlie walked to a spot in the ground. The shovel that had been lying on the ground next to the cabin was now stuck in the ground beside an open doublewide slab door. It left open a hole in the ground about four feet square. Captain Russell could see the loose dirt all the way around the hole where Charlie's men had scraped it away. The same dirt that Pap had used to seal the door to the hole.

The men standing around the hole all had their Government Issue handkerchiefs over their noses. Captain Russell started to speak when he caught a whiff of an odor coming from the hole. Quickly, he too, pulled a kerchief from his back pocket and placed it over his nose. He spoke through the kerchief, his voice muffled, "How do we get down there?" He pointed to the hole. Charlie showed him the short rope ladder that had been laying on top of the slab door, and was now barely above the wooden frame around the hole.

Captain Russell looked at the ladder and questionably back at Charlie. Using the ladder, Charlie disappeared down the hole. The Captain followed. By now, Ruff, Bill, and much of the first squad of rangers had gathered around the hole. The second squad retreated to the area of the outhouse which was upwind of the hole. Emma stood in front of the cabin watching. As he positioned himself near the hole, Ruff glanced in her direction and observed her somber face, one that showed no hint of emotion.

A number of minutes passed, and Ruff was about ready to call out to the Captain when his head and shoulders appeared at the hole.

"Here, Ruff! Catch!" The Captain tossed him a black bundle. Then in quick succession, he tossed out three more bundles. It took Ruff only a second to recognize the bundles. He stared at the Captain.

"What is it?" Charlie inquired. He had not seen what the other two had. "What have you got there?" Ruff tossed one of the smaller bundles to Charlie. Charlie looked at Ruff with amazement on his face. "Is this what I think it is? Captain, this is a bear hide!"

The Captain nodded. "They are all bear hides. Two adults and two second year cubs."

"Is that where the stench is coming from?" asked Ruff.

"I'm afraid not; there are also two grown young men down here; at least as near as I can tell. The bodies are about three time's their normal size." The Captain said, still standing in the hole. "I would guess they've been here two or three days. And in this heat . . ."

Ruff asked. "Can you tell what happened to them? Is it an accident?"

The Captain shook his head. "I don't think so. I can't see any marks on the older one, but the younger just about lost his head. It is barely attached to the body. Somebody, or something, really did a number on him."

Ruff looked at Emma and back at Russell. "Emma?"

Captain Russell shook his head. "Come on down and take a look, if you have the stomach to, but this is nothing Emma could have done. This took some doing." The captain climbed out of the hole. When Ruff entered the hole he tied his kerchief around his face covering his nose and his mouth. After only a few minutes, Ruff was back at the hole and looked up at Captain Russell. "It's hard to tell anything; they are so distorted that I doubt their own mother could recognize them. I couldn't tell what killed them." Ruff didn't tell the Captain that he thought they might be the two who held him prisoner at the campsite along the stream but he wasn't sure.

As Ruff climbed out of the hole, the Captain turned to Charlie.

"Charlie, get three men and two more shovels. For now we will bury these fellows where they lay. Make sure the burial detail knows to cover them well and then reseal the hole by covering the door. I don't want anyone or anything digging these guys up until the proper authorities have been notified."

"You saying that this could be my case?"

Captain Russell, Bill, and Ruff all three whirled in unison.

There stood Sheriff Crocker, trying to control his valuable dog, tugging and straining at the end of his leash.

"What did you say?" Bill spoke first.

"Well Larimer is my county. I suppose this is my case."

"But it occurred on federal land." Bill replied

"It occurred in Colorado. This is a case for the CBI." Agent Collins, one of the Colorado agents spoke up. They were killed on Colorado land"

"And how do you know that? Who told you they were killed on Government land?" Crocker demanded. Another CBI agent let out a chuckle. The Sheriff turned and stepped close to the agent. "Where did you say the State land was located in this part of the country?" Crocker never cracked a smile or showed any other indication that he was anything but serious.

"I think I will go have a talk with that little lady from the cabin," Crocker hesitated a few seconds to see if anyone would challenge his authority. No one moved nor spoke. "Trooper," Crocker said as he walked over to where one of the Highway Patrol Troopers stood. "By the authority granted me by the Colorado State Legislature, I hereby grant you a temporary appointment of deputy of Larimer County, which makes you an official of the County of Larimer under my jurisdiction. Do you accept the appointment?"

The trooper looked confused, but he was used to following the orders of others in authority. "Yes, I guess so. If you say so."

"Thank you, now if you will accompany me, we will go ask the little lady some very important questions. Do you take good notes, trooper?"

In his wake, Sheriff Crocker left a Federal National Forest District Superintendent, and a ranking ranger captain in command of two full forest ranger squads, both staring after him in total disbelief of what they had just experienced. Plus four agents from the Colorado Bureau of Investigation, and Ruff, all with their mouths agape, astonished at what they had just witnessed. The only member of the original "invasion force" that seemed to take it all in stride was at the present time pawing at the dirt piled up around a doublewide slab door. A drug-sniffing collie named "Boots."

CHAPTER 33

"Lif must git on." To Pap the saying had merit: Life must go on. If those who knew him could say nothing else he hoped they could say of Arnold Amos Stubblefield that he was a man of his word, true to his beliefs. Now it was time for him to keep his word. As the boys were growing up, he had always told them: "Ef'in somptin ever happen ta ya boys, I's haft ta take care of the one who done it. I's teel ya thet." He had repeated his oath to them many times. Now he was to be put to the test. Could he keep his word, or not?

An ache in his left arm caused him to shift the shotgun to the other arm in hopes to relieve the pain. It helped. Absent-mindedly, he reached down to his pants pocket to feel the two shells. Yes, they were there. Earlier, he had put two in the gun, one for each barrel, and had stuck the last two in his front pants pocket. He grimaced when he recalled the time he acquired the gun and the shells. He did it now.

Remembering the story was easy; dealing with it in his mind wasn't something he liked to do. It'd been what, almost two years ago now? He'd had three boys then, and they were a handful. Always scrapping between them. Especially when the two youngest would try to gang up on the oldest. Will had made them see stars more than once.

Pap's kinfolk believed it to be an unforgiving act to speak of the dead by pronouncing their given name aloud. But he saw nothing wrong in thinking of them by name in thought. He did so now.

Pap knew his boys and they usually got along fine during times on the hunt and this was a time of hunting, as they were setting out homemade traps, trying to catch some meat to mix with Emma's potatoes. *My*, Pap thought, *that woman loves to grow her potatoes. But she's stingy with them. Won't cook more than half a dozen at a time.*

They had been setting rabbit traps up on the slope of the high ridge when they met these two boys. They weren't exactly boys, one appeared to be about 30 years of age and introduced himself as Sandy Ritz. He said he was a salesman from St. Louis on a week long trip through Colorado. His friend, John Abbott, appeared near the same age and dealt in cattle and land speculations. They were just sitting on an old log, when Pap and his three boys came upon them. Pap could tell they'd been hitting the bottle a little heavy, probably more than one bottle, he also noticed they carried a rifle and a shotgun. Like Pap and the boys, they were also hunting on Government land, neither of which, the bottle nor the hunting bothered Pap none, he'd do the same if he had a gun or a full bottle. After introductions were made the conversation centered on the question of why Pap nor the boys carried a gun. Pap explained simply, "thay had non."

"Well," said Sandy, "I'll tell you what, if you are willing to make a bet, I'll give you a chance to win this old shotgun from me."

His youngest boy Little Amos, always quick of tongue, and it usually got him in trouble with Pap, spoke up. "Ain't woof much," he said. Pap grinned

"What are you talking about," Sandy exclaimed, apparently a little insulted, "you young whippersnapper, this is a fine gun."

"Fer squ'rel ma'be, ma'be not." Little Amos said. Like his Pap Little Amos wasn't one to turn anything loose easily. But Pap had a bad feeling about the two strangers and decided not to let Little Amos get suckered into something.

"Thet enough, Lit'le Amos, thay's got ta hafe somptin ta learn wit. Ya best git ta settin thet trap, now." Pap motioned to Little Amos and the boy knelt to rig the rabbit trap. John Abbott decided to speak up. "You' all need to teach the boy some lessens. He has a smart mouth. Someone's going to fix it someday."

"The boy talk the tooth. Thet gun's not woof much wit out shot. Ya got shot?" Pap said curiously. Later because of what happened, Pap realized his error, "I's should haft left well nough alone."

"If you could speak the Queen's English it would help." Said Sandy. "We don't follow your hill talk, mister."

Will and Ham stood together off to one side. Will at 23 years old had broad shoulders and surpassed his Pap and 18 year-old brother Ham who themselves were six feet tall, by a couple of inches. Little Amos at 16, had yet to match the other three, for his height was a mere five foot, ten inches. When Sandy made his remark the two sons separated and each took a defensive position on either side of the two drunken men. Ham placed his right hand on the corn knife that he had tucked in the waistband of his jeans; Will rested his left hand on the handle of his hunting knife. Will wore the knife in a sheath fastened to his leg with two pieces of leather. At the top and bottom of the sheath a leather string tied each end tightly to Will's leg. What Sandy and his friend Abbott didn't know was that Will could draw the knife from its sheath and fling it faster than the eye could follow. And Will seldom missed his target.

Sandy reached into his left hind pocket and extracted a bottle. Taking a long pull on the contents of the bottle, he handed it to his companion, Abbott also took a long drink that finished the bottle. Then tossed it into the brush.

"Another dead soldier," he commented, chuckling, "Now, about that bet. My shot gun against your string of rabbits, and an apology from the boy there, that Sandy can cut this tree leaf in one shot of his rifle from here to that tree over yonder." Abbott picked up an oak tree leaf from the ground and held it up. Pap didn't wavier.

"I's onlest got 'bout five rabbit wit I's. Thet don't sees like a 'air bet."

Abbott misunderstood. "Okay, I'll throw in the shells we have for the gun. I think I have about 10 shells all together."

Pap and his three boys grinned. "Dont meen ta be rude, boy, but ya done rised the bet. I's don't haft nothing elst ta put in." Pap was serious.

"Tell you what, if Sandy splits the leaf, I also get to box the ears of your smart mouthed boy for you. How's that for evening up the scorecard?"

"An ef'in ya don't?"

"The boy gets to try to box my ears."

"Wot ya tink boy? Ya en'tested?"

"I's like ta box he's ear, Pap. I's would like thet much" Little Amos wasn't one to back down when challenged.

"All rite then, Ya got a deel."

"Fine, Sandy, you ready?" Sandy nodded and replied, "John go set this leaf on that tree yonder. Put it where I can see it good now." Abbott did as he was told and Sandy took aim with his rifle. When the shot rang out, the leaf flew. Abbott retrieved the leaf and sure enough there was a hole in the middle of it. Pap handed over the five rabbits and shot a look at Little Amos. The boy stood his ground until Pap spoke.

"We'ens done make a deel. Ya apple'jiz ta the man, boy."

"Orry." Little Amos gave only the one-word apology.

"There's one more thing," said Sandy; "I still get to box your ears, boy."

"I's sed ya could try." Little Amos wasn't about to give up on that point.

Sandy handed his rifle to Abbott with his left hand and in one motion, swung a right on Little Amos's jaw. It was a sucker punch from the start and it landed hard. The youngster never saw it coming. His head snapped back with such force that Little Amos suffered a severe head trauma. The bruise to the brain was huge; it caused a massive build up of fluid in the cranial cavity. In addition to the damage caused by the powerful punch, the youngster's head struck a rock when he hit the ground. The impact of the rock fractured the skull. This second injury caused additional inflammation in the cranial cavity. The pressure put on the brain was just too much; it literally squeezed the brain until death occurred. Beyond the help of anyone, Little Amos slowly passed away. Even if medical help had been available, he would not have survived.

Pap went to the aid of his fallen son, but could not find a sign of life. If Little Amos weren't dead, Pap knew he soon would be. As they looked on in disbelief, the two drunken campers went into a panic. John Abbott held onto the rifle, but dropped the shotgun, and ran. Sandy found himself unarmed and out-manned. He did what seemed to be the smart thing to do, he ran also. Pap snatched up the dropped shotgun broke the breach checking to see that there was a shell in each chamber. He turned to his remaining two sons.

"Ya boys take care of ya broter. bury em deep as ya ken. I's be bak soon." Without another word, Pap started walking in the same direction the two men had fled.

The boys used their hunting knife and corn knife to complete the task given them. After they finished with the burial, they leaned back against trees and waited. Along about sun down they spied Pap coming through the woods carrying the shotgun in the crook of his arm. Walking up to the boys he spoke quietly. "I's tote ya fer, ef'in enny thin happen ta ya, I's take care of the one thet done it. Now I's wont ya ta belef ya Pap. The one thet put ya broter in the grave wont be doin it enny more." He stood before his two sons, clicked the lever, and broke open the breach of the shotgun. Popping out the two spent shells, they fell to the ground. Pap reached into his front pocket, which was full and bulging. He reloaded both barrels, and kicked at the two ejected empty shells. Then, speaking softly to his two remaining sons, gave a simple command.

"Sed be ta ya broter, boys, an let's git home."

Within minutes, the three men were on the trail to the cabin in the box canyon—the place they all called home even though it was located in a national forest.

CHAPTER 34

Reliving the story of Little Amos caused Pap's heart to ache. That was a worst ache than the one he felt in his left arm. Little Amos had been Emma's baby boy right up to the time of his death. Pap knew Emma always held him responsible for Little Amos's death, and in times of thought he acknowledged that she was right. But Pap could never bring himself to admit it aloud. Pap shook his head hoping that the movement would scatter the memories and make them disappear. Now it was time for the same chore again, except this time he wasn't after a man, he was after a bear. After the camp boy had been dismissed, Pap sat at the crude table in the cabin for the rest of the afternoon. Only the desire for food aroused him. "I'll et now." He said late in the evening. Emma dipped a plate of potatoes and greens from the pot. Upon finishing his meal, he took down the shotgun. Breaking the breach, which rejected the shells into his lap, he checked the inside of the barrels. They needed to be cleaned bad, but Pap wasn't in a cleaning mood. He shoved a shell back into each barrel. I's goin after thet bar first light." He spoke but did not look at Emma. She replied, "Lef the bar, it ain't goin ta do ya enny good ta keel thet dumm bar. He dont know nothin elst. He's jest be'in a bar."

But Pap couldn't let it go. A man's got to do what a man's got to do, he thought to himself, then said to Emma: "I's got ta do wot I's got ta do. Wot good the man wot ken not kept he's word?"

And Pap believed in being a man of his word. He had to settle the score with the bear. The easy part was in telling which bear he was after. *She's got the mark of Ham on her, yes she does. And I must find her and settle the score for Ham and for Will.* Pap frowned, disgusted with himself for thinking the boy's names, even though he did not say them aloud.

Pap, aware that the difficult part of any hunt would be finding the prey. Knowing that most she bears had a home territory where they searched for food, he also knew they would often move into an adjoining territory if a better grade of food might be available. The trail had been easy to follow for some distance because he was guided by the drops of blood that came from the wound Ham had given her.

But now, in the morning light, he just followed the animal trail that he came across where she had stopped to lick her paw and wipe the wound with it to discourage biting insects. He suspected that when she started moving again, the bear would follow the trail because it provided a better chance of finding animal food. Except for honeycomb, any type of animal food was a favorite, particularly if the trail led to a stream where she could fish, or to something that had died. So, for the present at least, Pap stayed with the trail.

Having risen before daybreak, Pap had left the cabin in a hurry. After checking his precious stash where he kept the extra shotgun shells, he found only two left. He took down the shotgun from above the door, checked again to make sure that both barrels were loaded. Pap was a man who didn't believe in assuming things were as they ought to be. Satisfied, he shoved the other two shells in his pocket. He threw a few potatoes in a rag, and stuffed them in his other pocket, then exited the cabin. Emma said nothing as she watched from the doorway, she had already had her say. Pap stopped at the well to fill his water jug, nodded good bye to Emma, and headed for the site of the attack. There he picked up the old sow's trail.

Having traveled out of the canyon and almost half a day down the trail Pap had just left the spot where the she-bear stopped to clean her wound, when suddenly he heard animal sounds on the trail ahead. An experienced hunter, Pap recognized the sounds as two animals fighting. Silently, he crept on. Using the protection of the trees and the dense under brush, he was able to get within sight of the action. It was two she bears in a face-off, each testing the other for the right to feed in the territory. Pap was unaware of which bear claimed the area, but knew both were claiming the right to feed.

To Pap's surprise, he saw the wound on the face of one of the animals and realized it was the one he sought. With the gun to his shoulder, he was prepared but the shot never came. There were just too many trees and brush between him and the bear. Before he knew it, the fight was over and the she bear with the scar on her face had lumbered off into the woods.

He didn't want to waste his valuable ammunition on the winning she bear, who was now stomping the ground as if to say: "This is my territory, and none shall enter without my approval."

Since Pap had the wind to his face, he slipped past the sow and hurried down the trail to try to catch up with the scared bear. It took him until the afternoon to track her to a familiar location. For some reason the marked sow had made a direct path to the small stream, Pap lost the bear's tracks but followed the stream to the campsite. He knew the place, it was the same camp where Pap and the boys had the run-in with an old man.

Pap remembered the old man because he had been uppity with him, and Pap had decided to take him down a notch or two. But Ham . . . the boy had failed to secure the ropes, and the old man escaped.

Now the bear led him back to the old man's campsite. Pap decided that the prudent thing to do was to lie in wait and observe the camp for awhile and learn what he could. It was even possible that someone else now used the same campsite.

Pap hunkered down to play it smart and wait. Pap soon realized he had lost sight of the bear, the thing he wanted most. A little antsy, and disgusted at his mistake, he asked himself an important question, *where did she go?*

*   *   *

Although the book he was reading kept his interest for a while, Mike soon became restless and ready for some action. Rising from his spot next to a large pine tree, he stretched and yawned. It was the middle of the afternoon and Mike thought of the cool water in the creek. Collecting some boiled and strained water from the pot by the fire pit, he filled his water bottle. He still carried it as a reminder of his days at the cabin. He slipped his hunting knife into his belt and started for the stream, envisioning an evening of exploring the streambed. Thoughts of Ruff suddenly entered his mind: *know your environment, it is your friend or your enemy. Be aware of which is which, for you may have to rely on it for your survival some time.*

Reaching the mountain stream, Mike decided to explore the area downstream of his camp. Recalling more of Ruff's lecture, he let his mind take over. *In being aware you must notice everything. What kind of bush is that? Have you ever seen an animal eating the leaves, roots, or fruit from it? Where does it grow, and how can you use it to your advantage? All these things are important for you to know about one kind of plant. And there are many dozens to observe.*

Wanting to explore the stream itself, Mike investigated the stream shore on the camp side of the water. He worked his way down the stream for what seemed to him as several miles, though probably a lot less. He found several different kinds of water insect larvae that he thought might be good fish bait. *Maybe I should try to catch some fresh food to eat. Wouldn't Ruff be surprised if I caught a mess of trout? I think there is some fishing gear in one of the camp packs. I'll have to check when I get back to camp.*

His wandering led him even further downstream. He soon realized that the sun was getting low in the sky and that he should start back. Deciding to cross the stream in a shallow spot, he started back upstream on the opposite side. Trying to notice everything that Ruff had mentioned in his lectures, Mike began to experience a different world. *I am actually enjoying this. It is fascinating to ask yourself questions about a plant, animal, or rock. Why is it here and not there? What good is it to me? How can I best use it? What can I make out of it? All these questions about one little plant. Maybe Ruff's world isn't so weird after all. I think I will do this again tomorrow.*

About half way back to the campsite, Mike heard what sounded like someone trying to start an electric motor, or something like that. He stopped to listen. There it was again, but this time he thought it sounded more like something rubbing against a tire on a car. Trying to be as quiet as possible Mike, slipped into the woods. He thought he knew the direction the sound was coming from, so he crept slowly in that direction. Suddenly he spotted it, or rather her, because he recognized the bear immediately. She was scratching her rump against a tree stump. This is a comical picture, thought Mike, scratching first one hip and then the other, the old sow continued for some time and Mike was enthralled watching her. Finally satisfied that the itch had been taken care of, the bear started feeding on some green plants nearby. Mike decided that he had pushed his luck far enough and backed out of the area quietly.

Only after safely following the stream again did he fully absorb the extent of what had occurred. *I observed a bear in the wild without her knowing I was there. I was able to move through the woods quietly and she didn't find out I was there watching, nor did she know when I left. I wonder if Ruff has ever done that?*

Making it back to camp well before sundown Mike set about fixing himself something to eat. He had worked up quite an appetite on his little excursion upstream. He decided to heat one of the packets of spaghetti and meatballs for his evening meal. Stoking the fire, he was able to get it going again and with a trip to the stream for water, soon had his meal heating.

He was struck with the realization that Ruff had planned well for this trip. The little packets of food were easy to work with. And most importantly, they gave off little aroma until they were opened—just heat them in water and eat. Quick and easy, that's the way he liked to cook. As he was waiting, he suddenly remembered that he had not replaced the food pack on the rope above the ground. He quickly took care of that chore and checked on his dinner. The pot was steaming. He gave it a little extra time so that it would be thoroughly heated. Then he dipped it out of the water and opening it, dumped the contents into a camping tin and began to eat.

CHAPTER 35

Unbelievable, totally unbelievable, that is what Ruff thought when he heard of the results of Sheriff Crocker's question and answer session with Emma. Ruff was puzzled with what he heard about the interview. *How did he accomplish so much in such a short time? Bill and Captain Russell had little luck with Emma, and here the Sheriff has almost the whole story in a few minutes. Maybe there is more to this guy than meets the eye. Never judge a book by its cover, isn't that what they say? Well, maybe I was too quick in my estimate of the sheriff. It just goes to show that people can, and often do, surprise you. The sheriff, who would have thought he had it in him?*

Having not been present when Sheriff Crocker interviewed Emma, Ruff had a poor image of the sheriff. If he had, his impression of the man would have been greatly altered. Unknown to Ruff, the Sheriff had a reputation of a bumbling unproductive oaf, an image he often enjoyed displaying. But when situations called for him to meet the obligations of his office he became a sharp investigator. When the clumsy fellow became determined, he turned into a worthy adversary. When Ruff asked the state trooper how the questioning went, he was told "the interview went something like this:"

"Here, Emma; sit down at the table. In fact, why don't all three of us sit at the table? There is that okay, Emma? Are you comfortable, Emma?"

"Emma, I am going to ask you some questions. You just answer them as best you can. Okay, Emma?"

"Now Emma, tell me, who all lives here in the cabin with you?" Emma reached out to the sheriff and touched the badge he wore over his heart.

"Ya the Mashell?

The Sheriff hesitated only for an instant. "Yes, Emma, I'm the Marshall." The trooper, who was there to take notes, gave Crocker a shocked look.

The sheriff ignored him. "Now, will you answer my question? I would be so pleased if you did."

"I's not know how ta an'sir ya 'qutchin. It's a hard one ta an'sir."

"Why is that, Emma?"

"Weel thay five onest, now jest one."

"You saying you live here alone?"

"I's did hafe tree babes, now none. Did hafe Pap, now no Pap, jest we'ens. Me an the babes out thar in the hole."

"How did the boys in the hole die? Emma, who killed those boys?"

"The bar. The bar keel em both."

"You're saying that a bear killed those two men? Is that what you are telling me?"

"Thet's wot I's sed. Don't ya hear weel? Ya wont me ta speak up some?"

"Whose Pap, Emma? Is Pap your husband?"

"Pap jest a man, an olt man. Don't haft no 'usman. Jest Pap."

"Where's Pap at now, Emma?

"Git the bar, I's rec'on. He's got a mis'on, I's speck."

"Is he hunting? Emma, is he on a hunting trip?"

"He's huntin okay, he's huntin ven'gce. Not ever weel he's find it. I's tote em so's."

"Emma, is he armed? Does he have a weapon? Emma?" Crocker leaned closer.

Emma nodded and pointed to the set of empty deer antlers over the doorway.

"What kind of weapon is it, Emma?"

"Oud"

"Loud? Like a shotgun? Is it a shotgun, Emma? Emma nodded her head.

When did Pap leave? Emma?

"This mornin."

"Did he leave the valley? Emma"

"Don't know."

"Thanks, Emma, you have been a big help. Is there someone you need to contact? Can we help you in some way? What can we do, Emma? Just tell us."

Emma stood from the table. She looked bewildered.

"I's got none. I's babes out 'ear, I's no Paps out 'ear now? I's got none. Don't know 'ear thay's be. I's none ta git. All's I's got now be ta tater 'atch. Jest me an the tater 'atch." Apparently discouraged, Emma slumped back down into the chair.

∗　　∗　　∗

When Sheriff Crocker came out of the cabin, he stood for several minutes while his eyes adjusted to the sunlight. Bill, Captain Russell, Charlie, and Ruff crowded around him. The Colorado Trooper was squeezed to the outside of the ring.

Bill was the first to speak. "What did you find out, Sheriff? Did she tell you anything?"

Sheriff Crocker surveyed the group. Enjoying his moment of glory, he took his time answering. "She told us everything. Everyone who lived in the cabin is accounted for except an old man she called Pap."

Ruff perked up. "What did you say the old man's name was?"

"Pap, I reckon that's his name, Pap."

Ruff grabbed Bill's arm. "Bill, that's the old man I encountered. The one who made me a prisoner in my own campsite. He's the one with the shotgun. He's dangerous. I think he might be a little off in the head." Ruff turned to Crocker, "Did he have any thing to do with the death of those two in the hole?"

"They were his sons, Emma says a bear killed them. Ranger Russell, you boys may have a renegade bear in your district. You might want to put out an alert. That bear could be on a rampage killing humans."

Ruff knew that a bear, not afraid of humans, was a dangerous thing. He also knew that once a bear tastes human flesh, they could become human killers. They can continue to attack humans, until disposed of. The sheriff was doing what he could to encourage the Rangers to send out an alert. All campers and hikers in Roosevelt needed to be warned about a possible rogue bear.

Yet, he couldn't accept the idea that warning the few campers were in the park was more important than pursuing the old man from the campsite. Ruff knew the man, and he knew that the old man was dangerous to other campers. And that included Mike. Ruff wanted to talk to Bill concerning the old man, and the possible connection between him, the campsite, and Mike. But, try as he might, he couldn't get Bill's attention. Ruff felt as though he was being shoved to the rear of the line of the priorities of his friend, and he didn't like the feeling. Not one bit.

Bill Waddle would be the man other people wanted to have around when everything went as it should and no problems hung over his head. However, no one wanted to be around him when he faced situations that challenged his desire for a peaceful day on the job. He could be a mild mannered fellow one minute and a raging rhino the next. This was fast becoming one of those times.

"Captain, I would like you to detail one of your squads to assign one ranger to each of the campsites that are currently occupied. Tell them to notify each camper of the possibility of a bad bear. Then follow the same procedure for the back trail hikers we have in the park. Make sure your rangers understand that they are not, and I repeat, they are not to invoke any panic among the campers. Make sure that the rangers explain that the notice is just a precaution. Have them tell the campers to continue to enjoy themselves, just be aware and report to the nearest ranger station, any bear activity they may encounter. Okay, you have your orders, Captain, why aren't they being carried out! What are you waiting for?" Bill demanded, showing his impatience to get on with other pressing matters.

Captain Russell knew his boss. Therefore, he knew that the last two sentences were not a reprimand of him, they were Bill's way of letting him know that he was finished with his instructions. He understood the urgency of Bill's directive and reacted with speed. Collecting his first squad, he relayed Bill's orders. The Ranger squad was on its way in different directions within minutes.

Once he knew that the proper procedure had been put into action, Bill turned to his friend. "Ruff, will you stop bouncing from one foot to another for a minute? You look like a kangaroo on a hot skillet. Just tell me what your problem is? And please stand still!"

Ruff opened his mouth. Then he closed it and a sheepish expression crawled slowly over his face. Opening his mouth again, he said.

"I forgot what I wanted to say, or at least I forgot how I wanted to say it. Anyway, Bill, I think that there may be a connection between the old man, Pap, and the campsite that Mike and I set up. I can't prove anything, but I have this feeling. My instincts tell me that Mike may be in trouble. He may have been the one following the old man and his sons up the valley of the box canyon. If that is true, then he's probably gotten himself into trouble. I think the old man may be after him. And with that bear on the loose in this area . . . I'm worried."

"Well, I'm glad you didn't lose all thought. Now, first of all, calm down. I don't want you to have a heart attack on me. One of the rangers will be investigating that campsite. If Mike is there, he will know enough to contact my office by radio dispatch. There is nothing for you to get upset about. Things are in motion and under control. What else do you think should be done that is not already happening?"

"We don't know where the old man is, and we don't know where that bear is. I don't like it that there are all these loose ends. What are we going to do about them, Bill?"

"Ruff, let me repeat, I understand your anxiety. You're worried. Let me tell you what I would tell any park visitor. We are doing everything possible. We have the situation under control. Just let me do my job, and everything will be fine. Okay, Ruff?"

"No Bill, it's not okay, I don't want your speech to a visitor, I want your speech to a friend. I want to know that Mike is getting the best service possible from his uncle's friend, not from a public servant who is just doing his job!"

"Now wait just a dag-gone minute Ruff . . ." Bill complained. He had worked with the public long enough to know that the best thing to do when dealing with a distraught patron, was to keep the situation under control, and not allow it to escalate into a battle of authority.

"No, Bill, you wait just a minute yourself. I think you owe me a minute. I'm sorry, Bill, but this isn't getting us anywhere. I want your okay to go after this guy myself. Can I get that from you?"

"Ruff, you know I can't do that. I don't have the authority to approve a directive like that. Not while I have resources such as Captain Russell and Charles Jones to call upon."

"Okay, then give me one of them. Let me have Russell or Charlie and we'll pursue this guy and find Mike. By the way, what do you hear from Lieutenant Summers and his efforts in the backcountry? I'll bet they have nothing to report. Isn't that right?"

Bill finally relented, more out of a way to rid himself of Ruff than of what he thought would solve the problem.

"All right, okay, I get it, you win, just go. Take Charlie with you and do what you can. But Ruff, remember the rangers will be pursuing this guy also. Don't do anything to get in their way. They have the Federal Government behind them, you have nothing."

"I have Charlie." Ruff smiled for the first time during the confrontation.

"Yes, you have Charlie. And Charlie, you have a responsibility to me, don't forget that. You keep me posted on any change in the present circumstances, you hear me?"

"Yes sir, I'll not forget that," answered Charlie

Ruff said, "Charlie, let's get things organized and we'll leave at first light in the morning. I figure it will take us most of the day to make the campsite. Okay, Charlie?"

"Sure, boss," Charlie answered, his face set in a hard expression as he moved away, and didn't see Ruff's grin.

CHAPTER 36

Observing the boy coming down the streambed, Pap couldn't believe his eyes. *What is he doing here? This is the camp of the old man. Can it be that they are together? Have they been conspiring against me all this time? Has the boy been leading me on, hoping to get the upper hand? I guess I better find out what is what here.*

Mike was cleaning his dinner utensils and clearing the fire pit of displaced rocks, when he happened to glance up and see the old man walking from the streambed toward the camp. There was still enough evening light that he could see Pap carrying the shotgun. Mike froze. Fear came over him and his heart pounded rapidly. His breathing increased, and in general, his whole body reeled in panic. He stared at the man but made no move as Pap approached the fire pit.

"Hay boy, su'prized ta sees ya 'ear. This 'ear ya camp boy?"

Speechless, Mike knew Pap was waiting for an answer, but no words came.

"Cat git ya tong, boy? Don't ya sees me boy? I's Pap. The one wot fed ya, member?"

Finally, Mike found his voice, "Hi Pap, I know who you are, I was just surprised to see you again so soon. I didn't know you knew where my camp was. How's Emma. She at the cabin all alone?"

"Emma fine, boy. I's sees thet ya fixin some food. Ya got enny food fer ya olt Pap, boy? I's gittin a bit hongree."

"I guess I can spare something for you to eat. Let me go check the pack and see what I can find." Mike walked to the food pack rope. He lowered the pack, and found another packet of spaghetti and meatballs. After replacing the food pack, he added a little wood to his fire and put the kettle back on the tripod. As the fire caught and began to blaze he added some water to the near empty pot. He leaned back from the hot fire.

"It will take a while for the water to heat up," He said unnecessarily. But thought he needed to say something. Pap peered over at the tent which was large enough for four people.

"Ya 'ear be ya own, boy? Or 'ear thar some one elst 'ear wit ya?"

Pap's question caught Mike unaware. *How should he answer? If he admitted that Ruff was here, then the next question would be: where is he? and Mike couldn't answer that question. If he lied and said there was just him, would Pap notice that there was a lot of camp gear for just one person? On the other hand, if he said he was alone, that wouldn't necessarily be a lie, but Pap might decide to take what he wanted from his supplies and Mike could be in trouble.*

To stall some, Mike reached over to test the water. He yanked his hand back. He tossed the spaghetti packet into the pot. Pap eyed him carefully, and Mike noticed that he had not laid the shotgun down since entering the camp.

"Ya 'ear wot I's esk, boy? I's did'dent 'ear no an'sir did I's?"

"I reckon I got the place to myself. My companion done left and went back to the city. Never can tell what people will do when they get out of their element."

"Wot ya meen, el-i-ment? Ya funnin Pap boy?

"No, I just wanted you to know that my companion was a city type. Never had been to the country or to a national forest. He just read books about the mountains and stuff, he never actually went to the mountains. He never fished a mountain stream, nor hiked through a valley before. And he certainly never came face to face with a bear. Your boys were brave; they never backed down from that bear at the cabin, did they?"

Pap scrutinized Mike's face for a hint of evidence that he was trying to give Pap the story that he wanted to hear, not what he needed to hear. Pap appeared to be satisfied with Mike's answer. Pap grunted a couple of times and then motioned toward the pot boiling above the fire.

"I's tink the food be good ta eat. Wot ya tink, boy?"

Mike quickly reached into the pot and flipped the packet on to a camp tin. He handed it to Pap, who made short work of the food. Mike made no comment about the ease in which Pap disposed of the food, Pap never asked for more, nor did Mike offer.

Pap stretched out on the ground next to the fire. Mike assumed he was just relaxing for a spell but soon heard Pap snoring. Mike decided to get some sleep as well. Contented with his day, Mike knew that it had been busy and exhausting. Soon both men were sound asleep. A large shadow quietly moved out of the trees and waddled into the clearing around the camp. The unattended fire burned low. The owner of the shadow had no intention of being denied; her hunger demanded food and she wanted sugar-rich camp food.

*   *   *

At last, things are going my way. The humans in the camp are not paying attention and the fire is not hot. Just the way it should be. Where there is humans, there is food, the smell came a while ago when I was in the trees looking for grubs. No smell now but it's here someplace. Must be careful because these humans are not to be trusted. Ouch, my face still hurts when it accidentally brushes against something. What was that? A rope tied to a tree and hung over that branch. What for? These humans they have such strange ways. Now that food, where is it?

Hey, there's a human lying on the ground. But there is no death smell. Why is he just lying there? Why is he not moving? What is that noise he is making? How crude. Who would ever grunt like that? He's moving, no he's just rolling over. Better keep quiet and look for food, hope he doesn't see me.

Oh my, what is this? It looks like an upside down bush. Except I don't see any roots. Some roots make good food. But it smells like human. Yes, there is a human inside the bush. Here are some metal things; they are hard as stones and don't smell like food either, rats. Hey, that would taste good right about now. A good fat juicy rat. Makes me hungry just thinking about it, Or even some ants or grasshoppers. That would be good too. But grubs and insect larvae they are the best. Huh, it's not good to be so hungry and remember about a few mouthfuls of bee larvae. Wonder if there is a new honey tree in the area. Something makes me remember finding one last year a few miles up stream from here. Might as well go back to digging grubs out of those old rotten logs in the trees. Digging grubs is better than nothing. Must find a better human camp, one with food. Sometimes it's just no fun being a camp bear. Especially in this camp.

CHAPTER 37

"Instinct, is that what this is all about? What is it with you and your instincts? And what about me? Am I just a pawn to you? 'Give me one of them, let me have Russell or Charlie, and I will pursue this guy and find Mike.' Those were your words, and here I am," Charlie ranted, "a pawn for you to negotiate with just so you get your way. Right Ruff? Am I right?"

"Now, Charlie, you know me. I say what ever it takes to get Bill to listen. In order to find Pap, and to find my nephew, I need you. You and I were the ones to lead the 'invasion force' in the first place. We're a team, Charlie; we can do it together."

"Like I said, I'm a pawn," Charlie made the comment with much less antagonism in his voice.

"You're a tracker, one of the best I know. Probably better than Lieutenant Summers. In all the time spent looking for Mike, he has come up empty. That's why I need you to help me. With your tracking abilities, we can catch the old man, and secure Mike's safety. Now you might want to get your stuff together and then get some sleep. We will be traveling hard and fast tomorrow. I want to leave here at daybreak so we can make that campsite well before dark tomorrow."

"You ought to follow your own advice, Ruff. You better slow down and get some rest yourself. You are not as young as you used to be and I don't want to have to play nursemaid to you on the trail. That's not what a 'one of the best' tracker does."

"You just find the track in the morning and let me worry about keeping up. I can keep my nose to the scent better than most of your rangers. You just make sure I'm on the right trail. Remember, that's what a tracker does."

Charlie was awaken the next morning by someone shaking his shoulder. "Come' on, Charlie, we have just enough time before light to

138

grab a bite to eat and a cup of coffee. Then we need to hit the trail. You have five minutes to locate the trail we want to take."

Ruff dressed in cameos and hiking boots, and wore his favorite wilderness hat, a broad rimmed reddish-brown number that he had gotten in Australia one summer. Ruff smiled, remembering *Mike hated it with a passion.*

"For the love of . . . can't you let a man wake up on his own?" Groaned Charlie

In four and a half minutes, they were on the trail, headed down the valley floor and out into the great expanse of the Roosevelt National Forest. Ruff had an old body, but this morning it was being urged on by a young mind full of vigor. Charlie, barely awake, was pushing to keep up, but soon, the two moved down the trail in unison.

*   *   *

Mike jerked awake at the sound. What was that? Who could be making such a noise? It sounded like an animal caught in a trap, and in great pain. Cautiously, Mike peered out the tent door to see Pap adding more wood to the fire, and singing a song that sounded like two cat's fighting.

"when I's yong I's ust ta wait,
on masa an hand em he's plate,
pas em ta bottle when he's git dry,
an brush way ta blue tail fly

OOOOOH
yimmy cack corn an I's dont care
yimmy crac corn an I's dont care
yimmy crac corn an I's dont care
ta masass got a way

'when he's would red in the af'ternon
I's feelow em wit the hicky boom
the pony bee'in a'mit shy
'when bitten be the blue tail fly

OOOOOH
yimmy cack corn an I's dont care
yimmy crac corn an I's dont care
yimmy crac corn an I's dont care

one days he's rid rond the farm
flies so's menny thet they's did swam
one chants ta bite hem on the thy
the devel take the blue tail fly

OOOOOH
yimmy crac corn an I's dont care
yimmy crac corn an I's dont care

Weel the ponny yump he's sart he's pitch
he's true ta massa in the ditch
he's dad an the yury wan'ded why
the an'sir be the blue tail fly

OOOOOH
yimmy crac corn an I's dont care
yimmy crac corn an I's dont care

now he's lie 'neath the simmin tree
he's ep'tap thar ta sees
'neath this stone I's fo'ce ta lie
the vic'em of the blue tail fly

OOOOOH
yimmy crac corn an I's dont care
yimmy crac corn an I's dont care
yimmy crac corn an I's dont care
the masass gone a . . .

Weel, good mornin boy, I's won'din ef'in ya 'ear ta sleep all day. I's needin ya ta fix somptin ta eat. I's pourful hongree. Ya hongree boy?"

Mike crawled out of his sleeping bag and put on his boots. He grabbed the shirt he wore yesterday, and made his way to the fire. "What was that you were singing? I never heard anything like it before?"

"Wot? Yimmy crac corn? Ya ne'er 'ear thet fer? It a favor'et of the homefolk. Ma'be I's teach ya the words."

Mike walked to get food from the cache and stopped short when he saw the marks on the ground. He knelt down and examined the prints below the cache, then called out,

"Pap, you might want to take a look at this." Pap hurried over and peered at the ground.

"Wot ya got boy, Oh, em bar tracks, we'ens had a vis'tor lass nite. We'ens ken track em this mornin a'fer we'ens eat."

Mike wondered if it was the same bear. *Why is she hanging around here? I'm sure that Ruff said no bear could smell the food in a double sealed pack. But she must still be looking.* He glanced over at Pap who was busy examining the area around the tent.

Mike lowered the pack and removed a couple of breakfast packets. Then quickly, as if a bear was going to rush out of the bushes and get it, he re-sealed the pack, pulled it up then tied the rope back to the tree.

Returning to the fire, Mike checked the water in the kettle. It was lukewarm. Though the fire didn't need it, he added another piece of wood to the flames. When the meal was over, and Mike made coffee for Pap, Mike got busy cleaning the camping tins. As usual, Pap had the shotgun within easy reach, and he reached for it now. Mike assumed that the gun was loaded, but because it was a shotgun, there was no easy way to tell without opening the breach.

I's rec'on we'ens best be gittin wit the huntin, boy. Ya got enny fire arms boy? Mike shook his head. "Weel then, I's geess this haft ta do." Pap stood and hoisted the gun to his waist. "Ya reedy boy. lets git." Pap started walking toward the stream. "The tack led thes way. So's we'ens ken sees he's tack at the creek. git a move on boy."

"I'm not going." Mike said surprising Pap; it even surprised himself.

"Wot ya meen, boy, I's mite need some help."

"I don't want anything to do with killing that mother bear. She's probably had her fill of humans, and she was here last night, I know that was her, and she didn't bother us. Why should we bother her?"

"She's keel the boys. Member thet boy. I's fixin ta git it, ya comin or non?"

"I told you, I'm sure she didn't kill your sons on purpose. She was probably confused when she hit Will. And Ham attacked her with the corn knife first; she just reacted to the pain of having her face and nose sliced open. I'm not going after her."

"I's ask ya non ta sez the boys name, boy."

"Sorry."

"I's left. Ya ken stay ef'in ya want."

Mike watched Pap move on toward the stream. *I want to watch and see which way he goes, up or down stream. Then I can go the opposite direction.* The old man turned upstream when he reached the creek. *I can't let him find her. Maybe instead of going a different direction, I should track him. If he finds the bear and I am not there, then nothing will stop him from killing her. If I'm there then maybe . . . yeah, I will give him a little lead, then follow his trail.*

Mike went to his tent to straighten it from the night's sleep. He noticed a piece of paper taped to the flap of the tent. The note on the paper was dated from the day before and the time noted. Recalling his expedition of the day before, Mike realized the note must have been left about an hour before his return yesterday, and he had failed to see it the night before. He read:

To The Campers Of This Campsite: This is to inform you that your camp area is within a large area of the Roosevelt National Forest where a bear has been identified as the one who killed two Park visitors. This bear should be considered dangerous and precautions should be taken to protect yourself. Should you encounter any bear, please notify the park ranger station through the telephone number on your camp permit. Stay away from the bear and it will probably ignore you. Do not feed the bear, repeat do not feed the bear. For further information call 1-800-555-3280.

Telephone! Ruff would have had a fit if I had even suggested I wanted to bring any electronic gadget with me. He doesn't even carry a cell phone.

"When you go to the wilderness, you go alone, you don't go with a contact to the whole world!" That is Ruff's way. Mom had once asked him, "What if you get injured?"

His answer had been given in a simple manner: *"First, you don't, but if you do, you deal with it." That's my uncle.* Mike mused. Re-reading the note it suddenly dawned on him that he knew what the note referred to. *The bear they are worried about is the one that killed Will and Ham. The park rangers are after the same bear that Pap is after; the same one that I saw yesterday. I know what Pap would do if he found the bear, I can guess that the Park Rangers would do the same thing. The bear has no chance. Everybody wants to kill it. And the whole incident was not the bear's fault. The bear is not a killer, it is a victim of circumstances that it has no control over. Pap and his boys started the whole thing when they killed the bear's two cubs. It's their fault, not the bear's.* Mike quickly gathered his traveling gear and set out after the old man. *I hope he doesn't find her, before I catch up to him! I should have gone with Pap.*

CHAPTER 38

Taking a lunch break would have been out of the question if Ruff had been by himself, but Charlie informed him that it was the wise thing to do in the long run; they had hit the trail hard all morning and they both needed a break. They crossed the valley and came to a small stream draining the surrounding landscape. It was one of the many clearings dotting the valley floors in the forest.

"This is a good place to take a break. If we aren't careful in our planning, we will arrive at the campsite and be so exhausted that further tracking, or other activity, will not be possible." Charlie said, "we don't know what we are going to find, so it's important we conserve our energy for any contingency we may have to face."

"You are always the one thinking with his head instead of his heart. I don't know what I would do without your common sense approach to problems, Charlie."

"Well, don't put yourself down, I would be thinking with my heart too, if I was in your shoes. And I hope I have your stamina when I'm your age. It's been work for me to keep up with the pace you set on the trail this morning."

"What do you mean, my age, I'm just middle age, not more than half grown," growled Ruff.

"Yeah, right. I guess I better check in with Bill or Captain Russell, otherwise you may lose your partner to a higher paid government employee." Charlie tried to make contact with both Bill and the captain on the radio. "I don't know if it's this cheap government issue or if the signal is too weak and I can't pull them in. The radio says that I have a signal, but nobody's home."

Forty-five minutes later they were on the move. Ruff and Charlie agreed that they still had a little over half way to go in order to reach the little stream. After that it would only be about half an hour to the campsite. They were making great time and Ruff didn't want to lose any more daylight than necessary. But, when one gets in a rush, that is the time that the unexpected usually happened, and for Ruff and Charlie, it occurred at a most crucial time. All their planning and effort during last night and this morning went down the drain. They were making a switch back on a steep decline, and they practically came face to face with the old man from the box canyon cabin. He had the advantage as his stalking mode put him on alert, and before Ruff and Charlie came into view, he had sensed their presence as if they were game to be hunted. Standing motionless beside a large oak, he was secreted from anything coming from the other direction. But for Ruff, he was on a clear line of sight, and with shotgun ready, and only five yards separated the two. On the narrow single file track Ruff, in the lead, came to an abrupt halt when the old man appeared in front of him. Charlie bumped into Ruff's back when he stopped unexpectedly.

"Hey, what's the matter:"

Quietly, and hopefully so only Charlie could hear, Ruff whispered, "We've got company."

Charlie glanced to where Ruff jerked his head and spotted the old man. They both could not help but notice the double-barreled twelve-gauge shotgun pointed in their direction.

"Hay, boys, I's not 'speckin enny com'enny. Ya lookin fer somptin?"

"We certainly are. And it might be you. You must have left the cabin and Emma in quite a hurry. Any reason for that?"

"Sed, I's know ya. Ya the olt man at the camp. The one who don't be po'ite ta he's nei'bors on the trail."

"And I know you, you're the old man who tells people what to do instead of asking them."

"Weel, I's eskin now, wot ken I's do fer ya boys?"

"You can tell us what you are doing with bear hides in your possession. You been poaching bear on Federal land?"

"Wot this word meen, po'chin? I's ne'er sez thet word."

"It means killing animals where they are protected by law against being killed," Charlie offered his remark, even though he hadn't met the old man, he knew of him through Ruff.

"Who ya? Hay, ya a over'met man? I's bet ya are. Ya wit the over'met ain't ya?"

"Yes, I am a government man, one who protects the animals in this forest from being killed illegally. You never did answer my friend's question. What about the bear hides we found at your cabin? How did you come to have them in your possession?"

"I's find them bar deed an I's skin em. Nothin elst ta do."

"You are saying that you found four bears, all dead, and you skinned them for their hides? Is that what you are offering in your defense? You just happened to stumble across four dead bears in the woods? Give me a break, surely you don't expect me to believe that?"

"I's thot ya boys would want the truf? Now ya got it, ya don't want it. Wot do ya want?"

"Where did you get the shotgun?"

"Wot?"

"I asked, where you got the shotgun?"

"Feelow gave it ta we'ens."

"What fellow gave you a shotgun?"

I's don't know he's name."

"A fellow just walks up to you and says, 'Here take my gun.' Is that what you are asking us to believe?"

"Don't care ef'in ya leaf me or not. It the truf."

"You better come with us. You need to talk with my boss. So if you don't mind, let's go."

"I's got bizz'nes ta take care of—I's ken not go wit ya fer now."

Charlie drew his side arm but before he could raise it, there was a loud explosion and the front of his body erupted into a bloody mess, and his whole mid section suddenly became an open wound. His eyes grew glassy, and he slowly he slumped to the ground. He never made a sound, except for a great sigh that came from him as he crumbled into a bloody heap.

Ruff stood in total shock. Of all the, daredevil stunts he had participated in during his lifetime, never had he felt the numbness, he was experiencing now. He had sky dived, jumped off a cliff with only a cord around his leg, ran the rapids of the Colorado River, in a kayak, and he even participated in a rodeo event once, but nothing compared to this. His eye riveted on the shotgun still facing in his direction. A wisp of smoke curled from the left barrel. The old man had not moved. He stood with absolutely no expression of any kind on his face.

"Wha . . . What did you do? You killed him. Why?"

CHAPTER 39

Just as Mike reached for the last handhold to pull himself up and over the top of a steep embankment, he heard a loud retort. He had heard the shotgun before and immediately recognized the sound. Oh, no, he's found her. He found the mother bear and shot her. Quickly, Mike's last step took him to the top of the high ridge, where he could see the entire area of the surrounding three valleys. He knew the shot had come from much closer.

Suddenly, he heard a voice, low and deep, coming from the trees ahead. The sound didn't last very long, and Mike wasn't sure of the direction, but he trudged on. More voices, and then there right in front of him was his uncle, Ruff himself, in person, not. a figment of Mike's imagination. He was anxious to talk to Ruff and greatly relieved to see him, at last maybe they could go home. Then he heard a familiar voice and froze.

"Hay, boy, so's ya come af'er we'ens. I's got a su'pise fer ya. This mus be the one who come ta the camp wit ya. I's rite?"

"Hey Ruff. What is going on here?" About that time Mike saw the crumbled body of a forest ranger lying on the ground. His chest blown open to a big red dot, blood oozing from a wound, his shirt ripped to shreds and clotted with blood and human flesh with many little puncture marks dotting the shirt around the gaping wound. The pattern reminded him of the shotgun target that Ruff had him use once. Following Ruff's gaze, Mike looked at Pap. He was standing straight-legged beside a large tree. The shotgun in his hands and pointed toward Ruff. Putting two and two together Mike believed he understood what happened. His eyes quickly spun back to Ruff. However, when Pap spoke, Mike's eyes darted back to him.

"Ya 'ear, boy? This the fren? The one wot got ya 'ear?" With a considerable effort, Mike found the courage to speak.

"Yes, he's my uncle. We came to do some camping but he got lost." Mike knew that Ruff wouldn't appreciate that remark. Ruff lost? Never happen. But something must have happened for him to be gone so long. He wanted to ask him, "Where have you been? I've been worried that something bad had happened to you." Pap's words interrupted his thoughts.

"Weel boy, we'ens got a pro'lem. I's need ta fen thet bar wot keel the boys an take care of hem. Then we'ens got ta figger out wot ta do wit ya an hem. Ma'be ya git loss in the woods an stave. Now we'ens heed back ta camp at the creek an figger out wot we'ens ken do."

"Hey, what are you going to do about Charlie? We can't just leave him here lying on the ground." Ruff said, his voice thick with emotion.

"Weel ya ken not tote em an ya ken not bury em, so's we'ens jest leaf em."

"No, you can't just leave him here like some discarded trash. Let me cover him with some rocks at least."

"Weel it take ya long?"

"I'll be finished in a minute."

Pap seated himself while Ruff, with Mike's help, used rocks to cover the body of Charles Jones from Chicago. Ruff made a silent pledge to his late new friend. *I will be back for you, Charlie. You will have a proper burial, I promise you that.*

When they left the area, the three men continued to follow the switch back trail down the steep slope to the valley floor. Ruff was in the lead, Pap bringing up the rear, with Mike between them. Ruff kept watch, and knew that Pap had replaced the spent shell of the shotgun. He also noticed that Pap only had one more shell in his pocket. *I wonder if that is all the shells he has? The two in the gun and one extra. What am I thinking? That's plenty since there is just Mike and me.* He glanced at Mike who was intently concentrating on placing his feet just right so that he didn't slid as he negotiated the steep incline.

The boy seems to be handling himself well. Like an old pro, instead of a youngster that when I brought him here couldn't set up a collapsible tent without reading the directions. Something else I have noticed about Mike, he seems to have himself under control and not a kid who is not sure of himself. Yes, Mike has an air of change about him, a change for the better. He has grown, becoming more adult.

It was well before dark when the three entered the campsite. Even threatened by the presence of Pap and the shotgun, Mike felt a renewed sense of security in knowing that Ruff was in camp with him. The first things Pap ordered Ruff and Mike to do were to build the fire and fix something to eat. Pap knew that the food pack would still heavy with food and Pap never let food spoil before use.

"I's hongree, I's take tree of em packets, an the coffee. an ya boys ken hafe wot ya wont."

Ruff accepted the task of building a cooking fire, while Mike busied himself with getting water and wood for the fire. Pap insisted that he collect plenty to carry them through the night. As Ruff completed the cooking chore, Pap took on the duty of constantly overseeing the job. His goal seemed to be one of making sure that Ruff didn't waste any time in getting the food prepared. He appeared quite pleased when Ruff finally announced that the packets of food were ready to eat. Pap finished his meal well before Mike, and gulped down two cups of coffee before Ruff drank his first.

"Weel boys, we'ens haft a pro'lem. I's git some sleep onlest ya mite haft other ideas bout takin off whilst I's sleep. So's we'ens weel tie ya ta each other fer the nite. Then so's we'ens feel safe, we'ens all be tied ta each other. Thet way we'ens all be 'ear in the morn."

Ruff admitted to himself that Pap did a much better job of tying knots than Ham had done the time before. Also it was interesting that to secure both Mike and Ruff, Pap tied himself to them. If they worked on the knots during the night, Pap would surely be awakened and most definitely upset. Ruff believed him when he stated his intentions for the boys to behave themselves.

"I's teel ya onest an thet's it. I's don't like bein woke up from sleep. Ef'in I's git woke, I's butt the one who do it wit the shotgun. I's tell you it weel feel a mite bad."

For Pap it appeared to be a restful night. For Ruff and Mike the knots were so painful that they couldn't get comfortable enough to sleep. But that was only part of the problem. Pap's snoring was certainly the best weapon for discouraging a bear from coming into the campsite. Though they had little rest but plenty of time to quietly plan their escape the next day. And so they made their plans.

CHAPTER 40

Untying the knots the next morning proved to be a difficult task. Pap in his hurry for breakfast was of little use to Mike and Ruff. He wanted them to start cooking the morning meal and he was all thumbs when it came to the knots. After about thirty minutes of work, Mike and Ruff finally freed themselves of the ropes. Their wrists were rubbed raw from the knots and Ruff wanted to apply some first aid cream to them. Both wanted to walk to the creek and wash up, since neither had refreshed themselves after returning to the camp. Instead, Pap insisted that the two immediately begin the process of fixing the morning meal.

Ruff wasn't in a very good mood. "Is that the only thing you can think of is your stomach? What's the rush?"

"I's hongree, an I"s need somptin ta eat. So's ya boys 'urry an fix the meel."

Mike, stepping around the tent on his way to the food pack, stopped short.

"Ruff, take a look at this. These are fresh tracks. And they are bear. Did I tell you about the note that a ranger left at the camp the day before yesterday. It's in the tent somewhere. Is she really that dangerous?"

"Yes, I know about the bear warning, I was there when Bill gave the order to advise all campers. But I doubt that she is really a threat to us. She is just a camp bear looking for some easy food. As long as we keep the double seal pack off the ground and closed, we'll be okay."

"Wot ya boys takin 'bout? Enny thin 'portant thet I's want ta know? Like when we'ens eat?"

"We were just talking about what to fix. How about flap jacks and cured ham. Does that sound like a winner?" Ruff's mood hadn't improved, just his attitude toward the situation at hand.

"An we'ens eat good." It was evident Pap's mood would only improve with the taste of food.

The meal over, and Pap finally sated, the two campers were cleaning up around the fire site, while Pap watched from a seated position at a nearby tree.

"Mike, I wanted to tell you that I was impressed with your awareness in spotting the bear tracks this morning. Also that you were able to differentiate between the old and new imprints. That's a good skill, where did you pick that up?"

"I haven't just been sitting around while you were away, which by the way, you haven't told me that part of the story. What happened?"

"It's a long story, maybe some other time. Suffice it to say that I ran into Pap and his boys and was detained by them. What about you? I gather that you have a story to tell also. I could tell on the trail yesterday that you knew Pap also. How did that come about?"

"Like you said, it's a long story. Maybe some other time. I caught Pap and his boys skinning out the old she bear's cubs and they decided I, like you, needed to spend some time with them also.

"Do you know what happened to the two boys?"

"Yes, I was there. I think the she bear was looking for her cubs and they just got in her way. I don't think she intentionally killed them. I think she smelled her cub on me, and Will was between us. Then Ham attacked her, and she defended herself."

"Why would her cub smell be on you?"

"I was forced to carry the pelt back to the cabin. It was a fresh hide and still strong with the cubs' scent. At least, I think that was it."

"I reckon you're probably right about that. Now we need to figure out a way to rid ourselves of our freeloading friend over there." Ruff nodded toward Pap. Pap yelled.

"Wot ya boys takin 'bout thar? Ya not panin somptin 'ear ya?"

"Yeah, we were planning how to keep you from eating all our grub up." Mike could tell Ruff was getting back to his old self.

"Weel, I's teel ya, it time ta be lookin fer thet bar. I's got ta set'le wit thet bar."

Mike turned to Ruff, and in a low voice said, "we can't allow that old man to kill the she-bear, it wouldn't be right."

"I agree with you, but you listen to me. That old man is dangerous. Don't do any thing foolish, you hear. I saw him shoot Charlie and not blink an eye. Remember what I said. He is a dangerous man."

"It's time ta git. Ya boy, ya take the led. Ya olt man, ya feelow hem. I's feelow ya. Enny funny 'tuff an I's got ta shot somptin. Ya git it boys?"

Ruff and Mike exchanged glances as they moved toward the stream. Peering at the ground, Pap peered at the ground and motioned Mike to follow the creek down stream. Mike was disappointed that Pap had chosen this direction, as he remembered the experience he had with observing the bear downstream a couple of days ago. Assuming that the bear was in its home territory, there was a good chance of crossing its path. How could he and Ruff ever hope to stop Pap from killing the animal if that happened?

The three were into the second hour of following the meandering stream when Mike spotted the tracks. Ignoring what he saw, the young man continued walking, hoping Ruff would do the same. He did, but Pap didn't.

"Holt it thar boy. I's tink thet we'ens got some more tracks 'ear. How come ya mist it boy. I's know ya sees them. We'ens got ta feelow them in sees 'ear they led.

Ruff never once looked at Mike, he knew that Mike had spotted the tracks and was trying to protect the bear. Ruff studied Pap, watching his every move, looking for something, anything that would indicate a weakness or flaw in his defense. If he had one, Ruff wanted to find it and soon.

Mike kept a sharp eye on the tracks as they followed them away from the stream. Apparently the bear had come to the creek for a drink and to immerse herself in the water as much as possible. Mike remembered reading something about how much bears liked water, playing in it was one of their favorite pastimes, and they enjoy just lounging in it. And they often find plenty of food connected with water. The underbrush became heavier and much more difficult to maneuver as they moved along the animal trail. They picked out a bear paw print, ever so often, and all three of the men were on full alert. The prints were fairly fresh and each one of the stalkers realized the chance of encountering the animal was likely at any moment. And each of them had a different desired outcome. One tracker was fearful of the encounter because of his concern for the welfare of the bear. Another pursuer wanted to destroy the bear to fulfill a promise of vengeance. The third tracker understood that no matter what happened, all of them were in danger of injury from a confrontation. Ruff also realized that the person with the shotgun held the best chance of surviving the encounter. Ruff's mind was racing to find a way to secure control of the gun. Desperation filled him as time was running out if he was to protect either Mike or the bear. He knew that when the face-off occurred, everyone's life would be in peril.

Only the bear sensed the presence of the others before they collided. With its enhanced sense of smell, the bear received advanced warning of human presence. This warning was not a soothing feeling. But rather a threat that caused the bear agitation. Its instincts were based on the conflicts of past experiences. Humans were scary. They were better left alone. She knew that humans could inflict severe pain. The bear had experienced this first hand.

Her skills of battle, developed by daily lessons of survival in the wild were vast and accustomed to being life or death struggles. She had defended the lives of numerous cubs from much larger and stronger male black bears, and from humans, and she had survived every battle. The battles taught her techniques of combat that had stayed with her now many years later. Her strength was greater than any human. But even she was unaware of its awesome power. Her survival instincts had been tested numerous times and in each test victory brought a new level of performance in battle.

When Ruff saw the bear, he immediately focused on Pap. Ruff hoped to gain control of the shotgun, and soon. As quickly as he could, he covered the short distance that separated him and the old man. Just as Pap was planting the stock of the gun in his shoulder, Ruff lunged for the barrels. With as much force as he could muster, Ruff pushed the barrels of the gun into the air well above the head of the bear. The sound of the simultaneous explosion that occurred from the gun momentarily deafened both men. Mentally, Ruff counted shells used. 'One.' But the recovery by the old man was quick and punishing. He swung the gun with its double barrels around with such force that when they caught Ruff across the temple. He staggered from the impact of steel against his skull. Mike, however, had not been idle in his reaction. As Ruff wobbled from the blow received from the gun, Mike lowered his shoulder and taking a half dozen steps to obtain momentum, drove it into Pap's mid section like a pro football line backer. The force of the collision caused Pap to release his grip on the gun with his left hand. With control of the weapon now only with the right hand, Ruff saw his chance. Still seeing stars, Ruff grabbed the stock and barrel of the gun and twisted with all the power the adrenaline pumping through his body would generate. The gun came free from Pap's right hand. Ruff stepped back, he had a clear space for the long barrel of the gun and pointed it squarely at the mid section of the old man. Pap was gasping for breath from the force of the attack by Mike. His face turned nearly white as he collapsed to his knees, panting like a spent dog. The old man grabbed at his chest with his right hand and grimaced from pain. Having seen the look before, Ruff recognized the onslaught of a heart attack. But he couldn't forget the face of the man who killed his newly acquired friend Charlie, in cold blood. For a moment, Ruff's emotion would not allow him to relax his grip on the trigger of the unexploded shot. The temptation to squeeze the trigger was great, but his sense of right and wrong eventually overcame the urge to seek revenge for Charlie's death. As Ruff watched over him, slowly Pap's breathing and color returned to near normal. He would live to suffer the consequences of his actions.

For some reason, as Mike calmed his own emotions, his attention was drawn toward the bear. She was standing on her hind legs, surveying the field of battle. The bear seemed content with the humans battling one another and satisfied with the outcome of the squabble. As the boy watched she dropped to all fours, rolled her head, woofed once, and with a surprising quickness, disappeared into the thick underbrush. She was rid of the scary humans. And she was hungry.

EPILOGUE

A year later on June 14th, the United States Federal District Court of Colorado in Denver, Colorado, held a hearing on the death of Charles Jones, Colorado Forest Ranger, First Class. The findings of the court proclaimed sufficient evidence existed to bind over for trial one Arnold Amos Stubblefield, address unknown, for the murder of said First Class Charles Jones. Rufus Brindle and Michael Anderson were two of the few people in attendance. Their depositions had been the evidence.

Last March, the Colorado State District Court of Larimer County, Fort Collins, Colorado found the same Arnold Amos Stubblefield guilty of the poaching of four bears almost eight months before, in the Roosevelt National Forest of Colorado. He was fined $10,000, and sentenced to three years in the State Correctional Facility at Cannon City, Colorado. Since his conviction, he has been an inmate at that institution.

In a related case, the Federal District Court of Denver found insufficient evidence in the case against Emma Doe of abetting a felon in the commission of a federal offense. She was released. Sheriff Benny Crocker of Larimer County immediately took Emma Doe into custody as a ward of the court. She has been placed in the Colorado House, a homeless shelter in Colorado Springs, Colorado. Declared a lifetime resident, Sheriff Crocker indicated that she will be assigned to the permanent kitchen staff of the facility.

On May 8th, a year later, Michael Leroy Anderson graduated from Colorado State University at Fort Collins, Colorado, with a double degree in Social Pathology in Cultural Groups and a degree in Biology in Natural Environment Animal Management Studies. In a news article of the local paper it was announced that in attendance at the graduation exercise were his Uncle Rufus Brindle, his mother Jennifer Anderson, and sisters Susan, Linda, and Jill Anderson.

After graduation, the article stated, Mike plans to spend the summer camping in north central Colorado with his uncle. In a statement to the press he stated with a mischievous grin,

"I also promised my three sisters a weekend camping trip in the wilderness around the Fort Collins area."

He has been awarded an internship, which begins in the fall, at the Roosevelt National Forest located in Colorado. He will be assigned to the Canyon Lakes District and specialize in Black Bear management in its natural habitat.